Who am I withOut him?

short stories about girls
and the boys in their lives

Sharon G. Flake

D1052054

JUMP AT THE SUN

Hyperion Paperbacks for Children

New York

To my nieces and nephews:
Denise, Michelle, and Donyell Wallace; Marie
and William Flake; Lisa and Joseph McCann; Veronica
Flake; Gregory Flake; and Tamika White. I love you all
and hope that your lives are always filled
with breathtaking beauty, love everlasting,
laughter, good fortune, good friends, kindness,
faith, and few tears.

If you purchased this book without a cover, you should be aware that this book is
stolen property. It was reported as "unsold and destroyed" to the publisher, and neither
the author nor the publisher has received any payment for this "stripped" book.

Text copyright © 2004, 2005 by Sharon G. Flake

All rights reserved. No part of this book may be reproduced or transmitted in any
form or by any means, electronic or mechanical, including photocopying, recording,
or by any information storage and retrieval system, without written permission from
the publisher. For information address Hyperion Books for Children,
114 Fifth Avenue, New York, New York 10011-5690.

This paperback edition was reissued by Jump at the Sun in 2007.
5 7 9 10 8 6

Printed in United States of America
This book is set in Deepdene.

Library of Congress Cataloging-in-Data on file.
ISBN-13: 978-1-4231-0383-7
ISBN-10: 1-4231-0383-1
Visit www.jumpatthesun.com
ILS-V475-2873-0 11293

Table of Contents

So I Ain't No Good Girl

PEOPLE SAY THINGS about me. Bad things. Momma says I give 'em reason to. That if I would just be a *good* girl—like the girls who wait for the bus with me in the mornings—then things wouldn't go so hard for me. But I don't wanna be like *them* girls: so plain and pitiful, boys don't even look their way or ask their names. I wanna be me. Ain't nothing wrong with that. Is it?

Me and them girls been standing on the same corner waiting for the same bus for a year now, and I don't even know their names. But I hate 'em just the same, mostly 'cause that girl with the red hair and gray eyes looks like the girl Raheem once left me for. She was a good girl too, so they say. She got straight A's. Worked in the principal's office, headed up the cheerleading team, and played flute for the marching band. You'd figure a girl like that wouldn't be no thief. But she was. She stole my man right from under me—for a little while, anyhow.

"What you looking at?" I ask the girl in the green plaid skirt.

She keeps her mouth shut and her squinty, brown eyes looking down at the ground. And right when I go to tell her she better not even think about looking my way, I trip over my own two feet. The good girls laugh—all four of 'em. Now, what they do that for?

"I should . . ." I say, going for the one with the red hair and run-over shoes.

She and her friends run to the other side of the street like they being chased by boys with bricks. I'm right behind 'em, with my fist balled up. But then, I see Raheem. Sweet, pretty Raheem. So I forget about them girls, and go back to be with my Boo.

Yellow phlegm flies out Raheem's mouth and onto the curb, right when I walk up to him. "Hey, baby," he says.

I give him a big one on the lips. "Hey."

He takes off his shades and eyes a girl passing by. Then out the blue he tells me to go to school without him, 'cause he's got things to do.

I push up against him. Stick my tongue in his ear and roll it around the fat gold stud I gave him for his seventeenth birthday. "Come on, Raheem. I skip English every day so me and you can ride to school together."

He yells at me. "Did I ask you to miss class for me?"

I snap out on him then, asking him why he's always wasting my time.

He hooks his thumb through my gold hoop earring and pulls down hard.

"Ouch! You trying to split my ear?"

He turns away from me and starts walking. But he don't get far—I don't let him. I apologize. Then I press kisses to my fingers and touch his warm lips. I try not to sweat Raheem when he gets a little rough with me or says he's coming over my house and don't show up. He's the cutest boy in school: an amateur boxer with a six-pack and honey-brown muscles that girls reach for even when they don't know him. I can't keep him on no short leash; but I forget that sometimes.

Raheem puts his arm over my shoulder and tells me again to go to school without him.

"No," that's what I wanna tell him. But Raheem likes girls that do what he says and don't talk back. So I remind him that he's got a test third period. If he don't pass it, he flunks the class. If he flunks, he don't graduate next month. "So you just need to take your butt to school with me."

He rubs the back of my ear. "I know you been waiting on me," he says in a voice so sweet my knees almost give way. "But I ain't going. I got things to do."

I can't help it. I get mad all over again, and it's me that turns away from him this time. He tickles my neck. "Come on, baby. Don't be like that." He kisses my lips. Says it's me and him forever.

I give in. Tell him what he wants to hear—I'll take the bus by myself. I'll do your homework, wash your clothes, lend you money, anything. . . . Just keep being my Boo. But then he takes off them sunglasses to wipe something out his eye, and before I say another word, his eyes crawl over one of them good girls, like worms sliding across wet dirt.

I am loud like my mother. When I holler, you can hear me up and down the street and around the corner. So when I go off on Raheem, people across the street turn and stare. "You my man! What you doing looking at her for?"

Raheem's hand smashes the words back into my mouth. "Girl! Don't make me . . ."

I apologize just like my momma does when my daddy slaps her. Like Raheem's momma does too.

Raheem says he's gonna forgive me this time. But I better check myself, 'cause he needs a cooperative woman. "Not a whole bunch of drama."

He's right. A boy like him can get any girl he wants. He ain't gotta take no stuff off nobody. "Sorry," I say, thinking 'bout how jealous girls be when they see me with him.

Raheem and me been together two years now. He my third boyfriend. The other ones, they was all right. But him, well, he's better than I deserve, I figure. I mean, like my mother says, I won't never win no beauty contest. But my body, well that's something else. *It's the Mona Lisa. The sun and the moon,* Raheem wrote in a poem once. It's too big in too many places, that's what I think. But Raheem likes it. That's all that counts, right?

Raheem don't never stay mad long. So a few minutes after our bus-stop fight, me and him are talking and laughing again. But when he bends down to wipe his sneakers, the good girl with the red hair and the dirty brown skirt comes back to our side of the street. She looks his way and smiles—just a little. He stands, she bends way over and pulls up her long white socks. He smiles. She winks. I go to tell him what I seen, but his eyes let me know I'd better hold my tongue. I do.

Raheem rubs my butt. "You know you my Boo. Can't nobody take me off you." Then he asks me to spot him five. Before I get inside my purse, he unsnaps it. Takes out my wallet and puts ten bucks in his back pocket, right when the other girls return.

"Don't be going in my . . ."

"What's yours is mine, ain't it?"

The good girls watch him kiss my neck and whisper in my ear. "Yeah, he mine," I say loud enough for them to hear.

The redhead presses her books to her flat chest and rolls her eyes at me. I point to her. Say for her to step into the street if she got a problem with me.

Raheem tells me not to be like that. "You the only one I want," he says, crossing the street, heading for the doughnut shop.

I look over at the good girls. The redhead looks

back my way, shakes her head, and just like that, I feel *dirty*—like somebody rolled me in chicken fat and left me outside for the birds to snack on.

I wanna give them girls something they won't forget, but the bus is coming. The good girls step into the street, just when Raheem makes it back over to me. He wipes white powder off his mouth with the back of his hand and tells me he'll come to my place later.

"Promise?"

He takes off his shades. Crosses his heart. "Sure."

When the bus finally pulls up, there's all this commotion, people pushing to get on. I head for the back, following right behind the good girls. A blind man steps on my foot. I tell him about it, too. Some fat woman blocks my way, so it's a few minutes 'fore I get back to where them girls are. When the bus jerks and takes off, I hold on to the rail and peek out between all the bodies to get one last look at my man.

"Oh no you didn't!" I say, digging my elbow into some girl's stomach. Slapping my hand up against another girl's back, trying to get to the front of this thing. But it's too late. The driver won't stop, even though I'm yelling at the top of my lungs for him to please, please let me off.

I lean over and stare out the window and see the redhead standing on the corner with Raheem. She must have sneaked out the back of the bus as soon as she got on. Raheem's all up in her face. Sunglasses off. Arms wrapped around her neck. His sweet, brown lips pressed tight to hers.

I wanna kill 'em both. But then my mother's words come back to me. *You ain't no beauty prize.*

The bus keeps rolling, just like my tears, down my cheeks and dripping off my chin. "Who I'm gonna be without him?" I whisper. I wipe my face clean on the bottom of my skirt, stand up, and head for the back of the bus. Then, well, I start thinking. Raheem don't never stay gone too long. Besides, he is cute. Really, really cute. And when you got a man like that, you can't be expecting to keep him all to yourself, not all the time anyhow.

The driver stops two blocks away. He eyes me. "Getting off?"

If I go after her, I think, Raheem's gonna be mad at me.

"Hey, you. Off or not?"

But if I act like I ain't seen nothing, he'll be by

my place tonight—like usual.

"Next stop, Seventeenth Street," the driver says, closing the door and pulling into traffic.

I sit down, cross my legs, and stare out the window. I'll go to his class, I think, and tell his teacher he was sick this morning. That he'll take the test tomorrow.

When the bus stops again, the good girls fly out the back door and head for their school.

I bang on the closed window. "You better run! Better not let me see you tomorrow, neither!"

The driver tells me to settle down. I let him know I paid my money and I can talk as loud as I like. He says something else, but I don't know or care what it is. My head's back to thinking on Raheem. Tonight, when I see him, I'm gonna . . . I'm gonna . . . make him something nice to eat, I think. And act like I ain't seen nothing at all.

Girl, Didn't I Say
I Don't Write Letters?

Dear Diary:

My name is Devita Mae. I am writing to you because that's what you gotta do in this class—write. It wasn't like that at first. At first all we did was talk. For real. The teacher we had was old and tired, and when we wasn't watching movies that didn't have nothing to do with class, we chewed gum, talked on our cells or to each other, and got A's for it. Then our teacher left. He retired. A new one came, and well, she ain't sixty-three years old, that's for sure. She looks sixteen. I think she's twenty-three. And you know what? The boys wanna do classwork all the time now. Raising their hands. Asking her to come over and help them with papers so they can smell her perfume and play with her hair—when she ain't looking, that is. And oh yeah,

they're writing papers all the time now. Getting A's
when they used to be flunking.

Diary, the reason I gotta do you at all is because
of Jaquel. He was trying to impress the teacher. So
he raised his hand and said, "Why can't we do
something different in this class? Like, I don't know,
write books or movies or something." Dominique (oh
yeah, she lets us call her by her first name) said
she'd think about it. She did. Only now we have to do
diaries (well really they're journals, but I like diary
better), and yeah, write letters to each other. I
laughed right in Jaquel's face when she said we had
to write letters. Boys don't like doing that. Only,
when she said they had to—smiling and just about
winking at 'em—they all pulled out papers and
pens and started writing like they were signing
million-dollar checks over to one another.

Anyhow, Diary, I'm not all that mad. See, the
teacher picked me and Jaquel to write to one
another. I like him and I'm hoping one day he's
gonna look at me like he looks at Miss Dominique
Dumar Dupree. (Sounds like a movie star's name,
huh? Lucky her. She looks like one too.)

Well, Diary, here goes. Jaquel and me are
supposed to write letters back and forth to each
other for fifteen minutes each period, and write to
you every evening for half an hour. Now you know

what's gonna happen: I'm gonna write to Jaquel just when I'm supposed to, and I will get to you when I can.

Nov. 1

Hey Jaquel—
What you doing?

Dear Devita Mae:
What you think I'm doing? I'm sitting in this class with you doing what I hate—writing letters.

Hi Jaquel—
Thought you liked writing—that you wanted to write plays and movies.

Devita Mae:
Boys don't like to write. But we like cute teachers. I was just saying that stuff 'cause when you do, she comes over to your desk and stands there smiling . . . wearing them tight dresses . . . looking fine. She make you wanna . . . well ain't nothing wrong with having a pretty teacher all up in your face, is it?

Jaquel . . .
She's married.

Married don't make you ugly, Devita Mae.

Nov. 5

Hey Devita Mae Calloway:
Can't write to you today. Gotta finish up
geometry. So don't write me back.

Dear Diary:
I'm supposed to be writing Jaquel. But he's talking
to Lisa, not doing math like he said. Dominique is at
her desk, grading papers, drinking expensive water
that I saw someone drinking on TV. She doesn't see
that the boys are talking or text-messaging people. I
raised my hand to tell on Jaquel, but then I put it
down. I guess he will write me tomorrow. So for now,
I'll just read the notes he wrote to me last time. They
don't say much, but I like touching the paper that he
touched. Smelling 'em, because some of the cologne
he uses gets on 'em after he scratches his neck or arm.
That boy smells so good!!!!!!

Nov. 7

Devita Mae:
Those your real eyes? I say yes. Mason says no.

Why are your letters so short, Jacquel?
Dominique said she will grade us on length
too, you know. Guess what? I saw this movie
the other day. The guy in it kicked this dude's
butt. It reminded me of the fight between you
and Justin.

Devita Mae:
Justin didn't whoop me!!! That's a lie people
tell.
    P.S. I bet your eyes are fake. What else is
fake on you?

Jaquel—
It's not a lie when you see it with your eyes.
Hey, I made a poem.

Devita Mae,
A sentence is not a poem. Here's a poem. I
mean a rap song.

> Devita Mae
> Got eyes of gray
> I see them every day
> But come night
> What happens to her sight?
> I think she puts them in a jar at night.

Girl, Didn't I Say I Don't Write Letters?

Hey Jaquel:
Ha! Ha! U r so not funny. Do me a favor? Stop
writing to me on scraps of paper that look like
you picked them up off the floor. And WRITE
ME LETTERS!!!! That's what we're supposed to
do. I want a good grade in this class, so this is
what we are going to do from now on. We
are going to write our letters in this here
composition book. That way things won't
get lost. Dominique said she won't read
every letter we write, just the pages we
have marked. So, write me a real letter.
Now!

Devita Girl,
What do you want me to write in this here
letter? I mean, I thought I was doing things the
right way. But you're a girl, and girls are
always trying to change us dudes. So I guess
I shoulda known something like this was
coming. The last time I wrote a letter I
was 10 years old and at Camp Roaring
Waters. My mother wrote me every day.
Sometimes I got three letters in one day. I
wrote her right back. Since then, I have
written one letter—and here it is, so stop
tripping!!!!

Jaquel:
I went to Camp Minnehaha when I was little. It was right next door to yours. I cried every day. I wanted to go home to my mother. They weren't supposed to, but they let me call her on the phone. And you know what? My mother told me to quit crying like a baby and go and have some fun. She wrote me every day like your mother did. I still have the letters. Girls always keep letters, you know. Do you have the letters your mother wrote to you?

Dear Devita Mae:
No.

Nov. 10

Hey, J:
Answer me this. Why do boys lie? Earle said he'd call my girl Marlina. That was two weeks ago. How come he didn't call?

It ain't your business. Mine neither.

Dear Jaquel—
Y do boys do girls like that?

Girl, Didn't I Say I Don't Write Letters?

Devita Mae Eyes of Gray,
Just 'cause a boy says he'll call doesn't mean a
girl's gotta bum-rush him. He'll call. . . . Give
him time.

Time? He had two weeks. That's 336 hours.
That's enough time.

Why you care? U want him to call you or
something?

Dear Jaquel—
Boys don't know nothing about girls!!!

Hey, Devita Mae.
Then girls should only date girls. That way
they will always get what they want, and not
have to explain stuff so much . . . and not
bother boys and try to make us act like girls.

Jaquel:
Here is what I'm thinking. Sometimes we can
write long letters, other times we will keep it
real short. Anyhow, guess what? I saw a girl on
the bus the other day. This guy was staring at
her, and told her she was cute. She licked her
lips and said thanks. Then she went over to him

and like five minutes later they was kissing—
hard wet kisses. People on the bus kept staring
'cause they knew she just met him. I was like,
girl you are nasty. Then my friend said, he's
nasty too, kissing a girl he don't even know.
What makes a guy do that? I mean, what
makes him want a girl like that?

Was she pretty?

Dear J:
She was pretty.

Was she stacked, Devita Mae? Top and
bottom?

Yeah.

Devita Mae:
There's your answer. A cute girl you just met
lets you kiss her—man that's living!!!

A nasty cute girl lets you kiss her. She might
have a disease. She might do that with every
boy.

Devita Mae:
I wouldn't care if she did it with every boy, as

long as she did it with me. Anyhow, who's
gonna turn down free candy?

Dear Jaquel:
You are nasty, too.

Devita Mae:
All boys is nasty!!!!

Nov. 15

Dear Jaquel Dickson—
My eyes are real.

What about your hair? In the bathroom we bet
sometimes. I bet that your eyes were fake, but
your hair was real. My boy Reggie said it
wasn't true 'cause your hair is too long to be real.

Why are you and your boys talking about me in
the boys' room, anyhow?

'Cause when you are taking a leak, Devita
Mae, you have to talk about something. Ain't
you sick of writing, Devita Mae? I am. So I
made up my own rule. I will not write to you
for the rest of this week. I will text-message
this girl I met in Chicago last summer. See ya.

Nov. 18

Dear Diary:
   The girl in Chicago is named La Donna. I hear she is cute. I hear she is smart, and that she's got Jaquel wrapped around her little finger. My friend Florence talked to Jaquel's friend Michael and he told her about La Donna. Florence didn't say it was me asking the questions. Good news though. Michael did say that La Donna broke off with Jaquel three times last month. Maybe she will dump him again, real soon. Or maybe I will just steal him away from her. I am cute, you know.

Nov. 19

   Dear Jaquel:
   Your boy Earle called Marlina. He talked for two hours. Could you talk to a girl for that long?

   No!

   You never had a girlfriend, huh, Jaquel?

   Plenty!!! Got one right now. And any girls that call me talk quick! But you're not that kind of girl. I see you in school—can't shut up, like most girls.

Yo, Jaquel.
How come you checking me out?

I gotta watch u. You sit across from me in class. Duh! Besides, dudes always gotta be looking. You never know when you need a replacement girl.

A replacement girl? You make her sound like an extra pencil. I would hate to be your girlfriend.

You would love to be my girlfriend, Devita Mae. Every girl wish she was mine.

Watch out, Jaquel. That big thing floating around the room is your head; too much hot air made it pop off and fly away.

Nov. 29

Devita Mae:
How come you missed school yesterday? Dominique wanted to see our composition book. I didn't have nothing to show because you take it with you every time. I'm not complaining. I don't wanna carry that thing around. But it got me to thinking. If I was at war, would I be writing letters all the time?

I'm saying this because my cousin wrote my mother recently. He is overseas. He told her he writes his mother every day, and he writes his girlfriend twice a day. He's a hard core dude. . . . Would kill you if you looked at him crooked. I told my dad the war made him soft as butter, writing all them letters, crying 'bout how hard it is over there. My father said, let's see what happens if you go to war. He told me I would be writing so many letters my fingertips would start to crack. "War scares the words right outta you," he told me. I got to thinking about the letters we write here. Guess my cousin wouldn't complain none, if all he had to do is sit in class writing to some girl. Beats getting shot at, I guess.

Hey, Jaquel.
I think it's romantic, him writing his girlfriend twice a day. Think about it. He's at war and all he's got to do is think and dream about her. I bet he kisses her picture every night before he goes to bed. I bet he talks to it and carries it in his pocket while he's fighting the enemy. I want a guy like that.

Devita Mae:
You watch too many movies!!!

Dec. 3

Dear Jaquel—
Thank you for telling me about your family.
Now I will tell you about mine. I am the oldest.
Know what that means? I do all of the work,
and get all of the blame. At home I watch
movies a lot . . . read a bunch too. My mom
and dad both work at the same job and do
all the same things together, like cooking,
gardening, and roller skating. When I grow
up, that's what I want—someone I can do
everything with.

Hey you:
I am tired today so I am not gonna write all
that much. My mom and dad have been
married for 15 years. Know what that means?
I was born before they got the marriage
license, ha, ha. I want a pretty wife. My dad
says I better want more than that. But he's old,
so what else is he gonna say? But I do want a
wife who is a good mother. And I do want
lots of kids and I don't want her to work. My
mom never worked. I liked coming home from
school and smelling cookies and snapping
string beans with her. You remind me of my
mother, kinda.

Dear Jaquel:
You asked me a long time ago and I didn't answer. So here goes. This is my real hair.

I knew it! My boy Reggie owes me five bucks.

Jaquel—
This is my real hair. I got more real hair in my bottom drawer at home. I never buy the cheap stuff; it itches. Ha! Ha! Pay Reggie what you owe him.

That's jive. See, boys don't know if a girl is real, plastic, or made out of wood. Why I want to spend four hours talking on the phone to a girl with fake eyes, fake nails, fake hair, and a fake chest?

Blame boys. If a girl is just her own plain self, you all don't give her any play.

Devita Mae Girl:
You gotta look good for me.

Dear Jaquel—
R u cute?

U know it. Do you think I'm cute?

You know it. What about me? You like what
you see?

Yeah. I like what I see.

Hey J—
Do boys have fake parts?

No! But we fake it sometimes.

Hmmm. How?

If we like you, we act like we don't. If we
want to call you, we play it cool and wait a
few days before we do. And if we don't like
you all that much, but like how you look, we
fake it—go out with you anyhow until we get
you to do like we want.

Jaquel:
Don't take this the wrong way, but you and me
. . . we would make pretty babies.

Devita Mae Calloway:
Don't mention no babies to me! I got things to
do once I graduate . . . like party in college
and go to grad school for my Master's in
business and open my own record company.
But you right about one thing—I'm gonna

make some pretty babies!! 'Cause I'm fine like that. But ain't no babies coming here till I'm done with my fun, done with school, and mak- ing big money.

P.S. There's some pretty babies in you too. Guess you got it like that.

Dec. 5

Dear J.
What you do on the weekends?

Watch TV. Play Football. Eat. Eat. Eat. Sleep. Eat. Oh yeah, when I ain't doing those things, I'm a junior fireman. Making the world safe. Ha, ha.

You probably start more fires than you put out. Me, I work in a bathroom at a club downtown.

Flushing toilets? Mopping floors? Gotta pay for that weave, huh?

Very funny, Jaquel.
I don't do toilets. I sell candy, mints, and mouthwash. Stuff like that. People give me big tips. Oh yeah, I give 'em warm washcloths for their hands.

Devita Mae:
Who wants to eat where they poop? And who
wants to spend 8 hours in the john?

Jaquel—
Saturday I made $50.

Who cares. Bathrooms stink.

You saying I stink?

No way, Devita Mae. Hey. What perfume
were you wearing the other day?

London After Dark.

Nice.

Dec. 8

Dear Diary:
We have been writing letters for over one
month now. With every letter I write, I get braver. I
ask Jaquel questions about the girl in Chicago. He
asks me stuff too, like if I had a boyfriend, would I
take money from him? If I had a boyfriend, would
I tell him I would only go to the junior firemen's ball
with him if he bought my gown, paid for my hair,

and sent me a ticket to come? Here I am, liking this boy, wanting nothing from him but to be sweet to him, and him be sweet to me in return (and that don't mean buy me lots of stuff), and who does he want? Not me, but her: Chicago, money-pit girl.

Dec. 12

Dear Diary:

Dominique gave us two weeks off, 'cause the boys are complaining about all the writing we do. She made us read some of our letters to one another though. Dominique loves reading letters, and writing them to people. And she wants us to feel that way too. "You can hide behind a computer keyboard or text-message," she said one day, "but the hand that writes with pencil or pen, always wins hearts, friendship, and love in the end."

While she was teaching, Jaquel handed me a note. I laughed out loud when I got it. It wasn't all that funny, but I was just so happy he wrote to me, just 'cause he wanted to. And before I thought about it I wrote a note to him, saying he should dump that girl in Chicago and take me to the junior firemen's ball. He looked at me like he couldn't figure out if I was fibbing or not. Don't he know I'm the one for him? Can't he see I like him, and I

would never do him wrong? I wanna tell him that,
Diary, but, well, you can't tell a boy nothing like
that. It would give 'em a big head and still they may
not want you. When is he gonna like me the way I
like him? Soon, I hope.

Jan. 23

Dear Jaquel,
What was up with you coming to my table and
sitting with me and my girls at lunchtime?

I was hungry.

Oh. It was nice having someone different at
our table.

Hey Devita Mae:
You bring all that food every day?

Jaquel, I like to eat. And I don't want to eat the
same thing all the time—pizza, fries, cold ham-
burgers. So I get up early and do my stuff
right—ham sandwiches, potato salad, cheese
steaks . . . sometimes my mom drops stuff off.

Girl, you did that sweet potato pie up right

29

the other day. Didn't know you could cook like that. Made me skip health class three times this week, just to get me some more good eats.

You let me know what you like, and I will hook you up.

I like a lot of things. Sweet things, mostly.

I see.

Do you?

Yeah.

You sure?

I'm sure.

All right, then.

Feb. 7

Dear Devita Mae:
This is personal. Don't go telling your girls.
Well . . . forget it. Girls talk too much.

Jaquel:
I would never tell something you wanted kept
secret.

Forget it. I was joking anyhow.

Dear Jaquel:
My girls were teasing me yesterday. Saying me
and you should be together 'cause of the way
you look at me, and how you wiped the may-
onnaise off my bottom lip with your finger at
lunch. Not even caring if I had germs or not.

Tell your friends to mind their business.

Jaquel:
You still with that girl?

She is hot, so yeah, I am still with her.

Dear Jaquel:
Why would you want an out-of-town girl? Why
not one right here?

Maybe I do have one right here, Devita Mae.
Maybe I got two girls, six. When you cute
like me, chicks be giving you their numbers all
the time.

You are stupid. Insensitive, too. Don't write me no more today.

Feb. 8

Dear Diary:

Today I got on the phone and called Jaquel. I got his phone number from his friend. Him and me talked for half an hour. It woulda been longer but a book I read said a woman should always get off the phone first when she is just trying to get to know a man. My mother gave me the book. She said me chasing Jaquel wasn't making him mine no faster, so maybe I needed to do something different. Now the book didn't say to call a boy first. In fact, it said never call first. It gives him a big head. But, well, once I got the number I had to use it, right? But I did good, I think. I got off when I wanted to keep talking. That's something.

Feb. 20

Dear Diary:

Jaquel dumped his girlfriend. Not for me though. He did it 'cause she was always out when he called, and she never phoned him back. I am glad she is gone. Now he will need a junior firemen's ball date. Guess who that's gonna be? Meeeeeee!

Feb. 28

Dear Diary:
  I figured something out. Every night I talk to Jaquel, only I call him. He never calls me. So this week, I waited for him to hit me up first. It was hard, 'cause I kept picking up the phone, wanting to make that call. My mother kept saying that boys don't like easy. "Make him work to get you. Act like you don't care." That's how she got my dad, she said. So I am here waiting for that boy to miss me. But I'm thinking, missing me might take him a really long time.

March 11

  Hey, Devita Mae.
  Your phone broke? You can't call a dude? I started to call you last night. But, well, something good came on TV and I watched it. Then my girlfriend called and, well, anyhow, I almost called you.

  You stupid, Jaquel?
  Why do I want to hear about her? Why were you gonna call me in the first place? To talk about her? Do me a favor. Do not mention her

33

name to me. Do not mention that you have a girl, period!

Devita Mae:
Is it that time of the month? I bet it is. Otherwise, why you going off on me for no good reason? I don't get you sometimes.

Listen. I am your writing partner, that's it. So don't be asking me about my perfume or talking about me in the boys' room or staring at my eyes. And you know what? I heard Chicago dumped you anyhow.

D:
Don't think we turning this part in to Dominique, 'cause we ain't. Anyhow, you were the one calling me, remember? And check this out—I don't get dumped. I dump. I got it like that.

J—
You take the book and keep it since you want to be like that.

Mar. 20

Devita Mae:
You are immature, not writing me like you

supposed to and not talking to me when I step up to you in the hall, at lunch or in class. I ain't worried. If I was, I woulda wrote you before now. But what did I do? Played games on my cell. I'm just writing you because Dominique told me she'd take my cell if I didn't do what I'm supposed to. Hey. My cousin is coming home. He's on leave. Gonna get married. I'm thinking, would he do that if he wasn't in a war getting shot at? My mom asked me a stupid question last week. "That girl you write to in class. When you gonna bring her home for me to meet?" My mom likes to get in my business, so I ain't answer her.

Mar. 28

Devita Mae:
You better stop playing around, girl, 'cause you about to not have no partner at all. And why ain't you call me back when I called your place? Your dad answered the phone. Didn't he tell you? And tell him for me, that the next time I call, don't ask me all them questions. It makes me not want to ring you up no more.

April 4

All right, girl:
You think I'm gonna beg you. Forget it. I
got me a new partner. Sharinda. She's ready
to step in and take your spot, come Monday.
You know what that means? You got four
days to get yourself straight. After that:
forget you.

April 8

Hey, Jaquel.
My dad is like that. If a boy calls my house, he
tells them they gonna get shot if they don't
leave me like they found me when they first
met me. He didn't tell you that, so maybe you
sound like you can be trusted. Thanks for
calling. I liked talking to you. So your mom is
still asking you to bring me over? I'll go. But I
understand why you don't want me to come.
And I understand why you would be mad that
she hangs up on that Chicago girl and talks
bad about her. It seems to me, you can do
better. But I ain't no boy. And I ain't you, so,
well, thanks anyhow for inviting me to come,
even though you ain't sure you want me to. I

think I will say no, though. Too many things
to do.

April 10

Dear Jaquel:
I saw a show the other day. A man wrote love
letters to a woman in another country for two
years without getting one back. He didn't know
if she was alive or dead. But he kept writing.
I never got a love letter before. Girls like
those.

Dear Devita Mae:
Y u telling me this? I ain't your boyfriend. Get
him to write you a love letter. Bad enough I
have to write u at all. Well not u, but bad
enough I have to do this assignment. I hate
this. Guys hate to write.

Dear Jaquel—
You suck!

Do you always have to have your way, Devita
Mae? I would never write a love letter to
a girl. But if I ever did, I would have to
tell her to burn them after she read them.

Boys don't want things like that getting
around.

Dear Jaquel—
That's romantic. Get a love note. Read it.
Memorize it. Burn it. Save the ashes.

Why would u wanna save dust?

Dear J—
What kind of paper would you write a love
letter on?

Dear DM:
I wouldn't write a love letter. But if I did,
I'd use what I had—paper bags, notebook
paper, whatever.

I want mine on pretty paper with roses
on it, or pastel blue paper that smells like
flowers.

See there, Devita Mae!
That's why boys don't do stuff like that! Bad
enough y'all want us to write to you. Then it's
gotta be on good paper. Then the paper's gotta
smell sweet—forget it. No love letters!

April 15

Dear Diary:

Guess what? Chicago is history. She got dumped. Well, first Jaquel's mom got on the phone and said her son wasn't sending her money for nothing, so she should stop asking. I asked Jaquel how his mother knew stuff about him and Chicago. He said him and her talk a lot. I like that. A boy who is close to his mom will do right by you every time. Anyhow, that same night he dumped her, he called me. All he did was talk to me about her. I ain't care. See, the way I figure it, one day he's gonna stop talking her up and then he'll see I'm the one for him.

April 22

Dear Diary:

Jaquel's mother came to class. He forgot money for his SAT test and today was the last day to turn it in. She embarrassed him, too. She walked right up to Dominique and asked to meet Jaquel's partner. We weren't even doing letters then, so I wasn't sitting by him. I raised my hand when she said my name. "I just wanna invite you to dinner," she said. Nobody else heard. Jaquel turned red, even though he didn't know what she said. I told him later on. He just

shook his head. But he didn't tell me not to come.
So I came three days later. I never saw anything like
it. The tablecloth was thick and white. The candles
were long and pink, and they matched the flowers
on the plates and the water glasses with the long,
skinny stems. I sat in between Jaquel and his little
sister, Janice. All the time I was chewing the
chicken and swallowing the pink lemonade I was
thinking, this is gonna be me when I grow up—me,
Jaquel, and our seven babies.

April 25

Hey, Devita Mae.
Y are you mad? Did I say you was my girl-
friend? Did I invite you to dinner that day?
No. My mother invited you. I told you I liked
the girl in Chicago. We break up all the time.
That's just how it is. Now we're together.
Stuff happens.

Jaquel—
This assignment is almost over. When it's done,
don't talk to me. And you know what? I hope
that Chicago girl hurts your feelings real bad.
Just like you hurt mine.

D—
I'm sorry. Some girls just get under your skin.

Jaquel—
I bet that Chicago girl is like the girl on the bus
who kissed the boy she didn't even know. Bet
she is kissing some boy right now, and you're
here waiting for her to call you on your cell or
go to that ball with you. Boys get just what they
deserve, 'cause when you are mean and stupid,
why shouldn't bad things happen to you?

April 29

Jaquel:
I talked to Dominique. I told her we didn't have
no more stuff to write about. She said we can
finish up early, and do silent reading till this is
over next week. That works for me.

Devita Mae Calloway:
Why can't girls keep their emotions out of
stuff? We don't have to write about you and
me. We can write about other things like that
new movie that just opened up.

J—
I thought you didn't like to write. So quit
writing me. This is my last letter to you. And
while I'm writing it, let me tell you a few things.
I am an A student. I am on the softball and
tennis teams, in case you didn't know. I
am cute and I can have any boy I like, but
I like you. Only, you know something? I ain't
always gonna like you, so you better figure this
thing out quick. I'm giving you one last chance
to choose me.

Devita Mae—
You can't bum-rush no dude. I got me a girl.
You just my friend. And if you don't wanna be
my friend, oh well.

J—
Oh well! Don't write me no more. Don't call
me no more. Don't speak to me in class. Don't
come crying to me when Chicago drops you
like a pack of crackers crawling with ants.

May 15

Dear Diary:
Dominique says she is collecting our letters and
diaries in two weeks. You know what that means? I

will have to start a new diary. That's the one I will
turn in, not this one. Dominique don't have to know
all my business. Besides, I don't want nobody reading
my thoughts on Jaquel. He and me still ain't speaking.

May 31

Dear Diary—
    Guess what? Jaquel's mother called me. Well,
that's not what really happened. I saw her in the
store. She came over to me and asked me to come
to dinner again. I said no. That's all I said. It was
she who said she was glad Chicago was out of the
picture and that she always liked me best. Then she
asked how come I never call their house. I told her
I was not chasing Jaquel no more. She winked. Said
that was good. "Sometimes a girl needs to step back
and let a boy see what he's missing."
    I liked what she said, only me stepping back
hasn't changed things all that much. Jaquel only
waves to me. I told her that. Then she told me
something I didn't know. "Almost every night he's
got something to say about you."
    I didn't believe her until she told me about how
my father grills boys and how the other day when I
raised my hand in class to ask a question, my sleeve
pulled back and everybody could see I hadn't

shaved for a long time. That embarrassed me. "If he
likes me," I told her, "then he's gonna have to say
something. I am tired of him hurting my feelings all
the time."

I guess his mother said something to him, 'cause
a few days later he sat down next to me in class,
which he never does no more. And he talked to me.
We both got a B+ on our project. Two days later, him
and me were standing outside talking. He's been
nice to me ever since. There's no more letters, just
him and me talking, in person, on the phone, that
kind of thing.

June 14

Dear Diary Girl:

Since I bought another diary to hand in, I
wanted you to feel special 'cause we've been
together since I started writing down my feelings for
Jaquel. So I hope you like your new name. A lot of
things have happened in the last two weeks. Me and
Jaquel sat down outside of school and talked real
good. He apologized for being mean to me all the
time. And he said he was finished with Chicago. I
was right about to tell him he was stupid for hanging
in there so long, when I thought of something from
the book. You gotta make a boy feel good about
who he is. So I told him in my sweetest voice that it

was her loss, not his. I told my mother the other day that I didn't like that book so much, anymore. It never says what a boy should be doing for you. My mother says that's what she and my dad are here for, to let me know that a boy should respect me, stop when I tell him to, and make me feel special by doing nice things for me. I didn't want to hear all that, but she told me anyhow.

But, you know what? Jaquel was sweet to me that day we were together. He was standing so close, he made me sweat. And he asked me if I wanted to go a movie and out to eat on Saturday night. You know, I think he is shy sometimes. He was staring at his feet, almost the whole time. But when he did look up, and stare in my eyes, he kept licking his lips with his tongue, like they were dry. And sometimes he would push me, a little, with his elbow. I almost kissed him, you know. I almost just pulled him to me and kissed those big, pink lips of his for the longest time. Only I stopped myself. 'Cause I'm making him want me; not throwing me at him. But when we kiss, oh my goodness, the earth's gonna shake.

June 15

Devita Mae—
We don't have to write no more, so what's up with the letters?

45

Jaquel,
I just wanted to thank you for taking me out. I had a nice time.

D Girl—
You told me that.

J . . .
I wanted to ask you something. Only writing it down seemed like the best way to do it.

All right. Ask.

If u wrote a love letter to a girl, what would u say?

Oh God.

Just answer the question, please.

I would never write one.

'Cause you can't?

No.

'Cause you scared?

Girl, Didn't I Say I Don't Write Letters?

No.

Why then?

Drop it. Y can't girls just drop things?

Dear Jaquel,
If I wrote a love letter to a boy, here's what it would say:
My Sweet Jaquel, I like you. I think you are funny, cute, and got the sweetest lips. I like sitting next to you. You make me want to touch your hand and be someplace quiet with you. I think sometimes, "Does Jaquel like me the way I like him?"
That's what I would write in my letter. What do you think?

Dear Devita Mae:
I do not write love letters.

Oh.

June 18

Dear Devita Mae Calloway:
I hate to write. But you are back to not talking

to me and ignoring me so here goes. I do not
write love letters to girls. But if I wrote one, I
would say, Dear Devita Mae: Girl, you are
fine. And them eyes, man they something else.
When you look at me and bat them long
lashes, Girl, I ain't saying what I be feeling.
Cute is the best part of you—but not the only
good thing about you. You don't let me boss
you—I like that. But you ain't no dude neither,
and you ain't after my money. I can tell, 'cause
you're not all the time begging for my change.
This ain't no love letter, you know, but it's a
note. . . . Something for you to burn when
you're done reading it.

Jaquel,
I like you a lot, and I am glad you are not the
kind of boy who thinks giving a girl what she
wants is a bad thing.

Dear Devita Mae:
I like you too. But don't think I'm gonna keep
writing you after today is done.

Okay.

Good.

48

Girl, Didn't I Say I Don't Write Letters?

Jaquel,
Maybe you could write me every once in a
while, on special occasions, like on my birthday
and once every other month.

Devita Mae, Eyes of Gray.
You better burn them letters if I write 'em,
okay?

I will burn the letters and save the ashes.

Okay, Devita Mae.
Then I will keep writing you letters. Nothing
long, just notes.

Just notes.

Just for you.

The Ugly One

THEY CALL ME THE ugly one—the boys do, anyhow. The girls call me Marbles, because of the bumps on my face, I guess. My grandmother tells me not to worry. That one day I will grow up and be beautiful, like the ugly duckling in the book. But she don't tell me what to do now, while I'm still ugly, and all by myself.

They transferred me here to Mulligan High last year, in the second half of my freshman year. The principal said it only made sense, 'cause he couldn't make the kids stop bothering me. And he was tired of my grandmother and my father coming up there all the time, "raising Cain."

Mulligan ain't so bad, I guess. Maybe that's 'cause I keep my mouth shut. Don't answer questions when teachers call on me, or finish tests before the rest of the class. But I keep my grades up, no matter what. So far, I got a 3.98 average. My little brother says that's 'cause I don't have no friends. "Just books to keep you company." He's right. Only I never tell him that.

My name is Asia Calloway. I am just a regular girl. Not too tall. Not too short. Not fat, or skinny, or nothing. If it wasn't for my face, people would not even remember my name. But this thing—this face—gets me noticed everywhere I go. And all I want to be is invisible—to curl up like a dot at the end of a sentence and disappear.

I was born pretty, that's what Grandma tells me anyhow. "You had shiny black chicken feathers for hair," she'll say, rubbing the soft hair on my head. "And skin the color of piecrust baked just so."

Then something happened. Bumps—boils popped up on my face like bubbles in a witch's brew. I was seven when the first one came. Ten when the doctors finally figured out what went wrong.

"Don't worry," Grandmother says. "They gonna find a cure for it, by and by."

No they won't. Even I know that.

I never miss a day of school, 'cause once school's out, it's me in my room all by myself. So rain or shine, I'm here. Like today. Even if nobody but the teachers talk to me.

"Out the way," a girl says, pushing past me when I get off the bus.

I apologize, even though it's not my fault.

"Hey, Asia," Nock says, walking over to me.

He's with three friends, and smiling at me way too much. I know what that means—trouble. I walk a little faster.

Nock yells for me like he's calling plays on the football field. "ASIA!"

I stand in place. Squeeze my books to my chest, and watch my fingertips turn white.

Nock's hairy brown arm slides over my shoulder. I close my eyes for just a minute and pretend he's Ramon.

"Asia Calloway, why you ignoring me, girl?"

I've never been held by a real boy before. So even though Nock's staring at my bumps like some gross experiment he's got to work on in chemistry class, I am kind of happy inside.

"Yo, ugly," a boy says, throwing a Tootsie Pop wrapper at me.

Nock gives him five. "Hey, Ug—Asia. You going to prom tonight?" he asks, laughing just a little.

I shake my head no.

Nock tickles my ear with his fat, flat thumb. Then whispers, "Yeah, you is. With one of them, right?" He points.

His friends talk all at once. "Naw, man, I ain't taking her."

"She a dog, man. Ruff! Ruff! Give a dog a bone," one kid says, throwing a big thick pencil my way.

Nock's fingers pull at my long black hair. He shakes his head and spits. "God gives you good hair like this, and a face like that. It don't seem right. Do it?"

My left foot moves. My right foot follows.

Nock gets mad. "I tell you to go, girl?"

I look around. More kids are pressing in on me. "No," I say, taking two more giant steps.

Nock is knock-kneed—that's how he got his nickname. When he moves toward me, his jeans rub together.

"Yo, Nock," a boy in the crowd yells. "You take her to prom, man. You be beauty, she be the beast."

They all laugh, even the janitor just picking up leaves under the dogwood tree.

Nock's girlfriend, Nicole, comes over. She tells him that she should drop him just for talking to something like me.

I put my head down and walk into the crowd. They part like sliced butter, 'cause they afraid they gonna get what I got.

"Ill," people say, like looking at me makes 'em sick to the stomach.

And even though I know better, I rub my hand across my lumpy face and slide it through one girl's long brown hair. I pat another boy on the cheek, just when he's trying to get out my way. I reach back as far as I can and pinch Nock's girlfriend's arm. Then I run just as fast as I can.

"The principal called," my grandmother says when I get home.

"I know."

"Said you attacked some kids. Just like you used to do in the other school."

I throw my books down on the table. Jump up and sit down on the cold, green kitchen counter. "If they wasn't so stupid they would know what I got ain't catching, just ugly."

My grandmother's arms jiggle, like Nicole's fat booty, when she lifts 'em and points to me. "How many schools you been to now, gal?"

My baby brother, Barley, walks in the room and answers for me. "Seven." He holds up five fingers and his thumbs. "I bet it's gonna be eleven by the time you graduate."

I jump to the floor. Watch my grandmother shake her head. "Lord. What I'm gonna do with that girl?"

Before I answer, Barley puts in his two cents. "Just 'cause you ugly, don't mean you can't have friends."

The chair creaks like it's breaking when my grandmother leans over and smacks Barley across the mouth.

"I just meant . . ." Barley says, running to me with his arms out.

He's squeezing the blood outta me. I'm staring at myself in the metal paper towel holder. *It's a ugly face. He ain't lying about that.*

Barley is nine years old. Too big to be picked up. I do it anyhow. "Shhhh. I know what you was trying to say."

He twists my long curls around his finger like spaghetti on a fork. "I mean . . . you gotta be 'specially nice to people, if you want 'em to like you." He looks up at me. "Treat 'em like you do me."

I put Barley down and head for my room. My grandmother says I better call my father at work and tell him what happened. He knows, I say. He knows it was coming, anyhow.

I go in my room and lock the door behind me. Cut on the TV. Cut on the stereo. Close the lavender shades. Yell at Barley when he turns the knob and asks to come in here with me.

I lie across the bed. And even with the music on I can hear Ramon's soft voice. *You know I'm taking you to the prom tonight,* he says.

I kneel down by my bed. Pull back the pink, flowered spread and grab magazines from under the bed. "I know," I say, turning to page twenty-seven and kissing Ramon on the lips.

Ramon is not Hispanic like you might think. He is Jamaican. He's studying to be a lawyer. He's too old for me, really. I tell him that. But he won't listen.

Wear the yellow dress, he says. *The one your granny bought you for your cousin's summer wedding.*

I run to the closet. Pull off my jeans. Pull the

dress over my head and do circles in the mirror when I see how pretty I am.

"How should I wear my hair, Ramon?"

I close my eyes. He starts to hum. Then yellow roses and white daises float off the bedspread and cover my hair like a hundred butterflies.

Oh, baby girl, Ramon says, holding me close. *A thousand Hawaiian hula girls couldn't compare to you.*

I shake my head. Feel my wavy hair dance and fall and bounce on my nose and cheeks like sweet, pretty petals from a magnolia tree. My eyes open wide. "I hate my face, Ramon." I lean into the mirror and watch my lips curl under. "Everybody hates my face."

Let's dance, he says.

"No."

He whispers. *In here you are the most beautiful girl in the world. The love of my life.*

My fingers find his big brown lips. They roll over his long blond dreads and stop at his hands. "In here . . ."

He interrupts me. *In here, you belong to me.*

"But I . . ."

Ramon raises his voice. *And I won't let anybody hurt you . . . or be mean to you. Or say that word I hate.*

I look in the mirror. "Ugly," I say.

His voice goes low and deep. *Kiss me.*

I lean over and press my lips to his.

Again, he says, touching my beautiful hair. Holding me tight.

I go to the stereo and turn up the music. He is telling me a funny joke and saying he will be jealous if I dance with anyone else tonight. I tell him not to worry; I'm saving all my dances for him.

"I like that shirt on you," I say, coming back to him.

He looks at his chest. Points. *Mango,* he says, patting my nose. *My favorite—*

"Color," I say, then I remind him that mango is a fruit, not a color. He doesn't care, he says, because in here, we make the rules.

Mookie in Love

IT WASN'T MY FAULT. Girls just naturally take to my cousin Mookie, even when I warn 'em not to. So it's no wonder Shanna didn't listen when I told her to stay clear of him. "Mookie's spoiled," I said. "Spoiled rotten by women old enough to know better." But even I started feeling sorry for Mookie and Shanna after my aunt, mother, and all her nutty sisters set their minds to breaking those two up. But then Mookie shoulda known, when the Walker women want something to end, they will do anything, I mean anything, to make sure it does.

It started ten months ago. Me and Shanna was in the kitchen eating barbecued pork rinds when my cousin Mookie walked in. He thinks he's cool. So soon as he seen her, he pulled up a chair and took a pork rind out her hand. "Hey, cutie," he said, looking her up and down.

I popped him on the head. "Stop disrespecting my friend like that."

Shanna crossed her legs and laughed. "Who you?"

I told Shanna she did not want to meet Mookie. "Ten girlfriends today. Ten more tomorrow," I said, pushing the bag of rinds his way.

My mother walked in. She opened the fridge and sat a bottle of pop in front of Mookie. "What else you want, baby?"

Mookie looked at Shanna. "Something sweet," he said.

Mookie is a spoiled brat. The only boy born to our family for three generations. Whatever he wants, he gets.

"Dinner's gonna be ready in half an hour," Momma said, pouring his pop into a glass. Opening the freezer and getting ice. "You staying, right?"

I snatched his glass and drank his pop. "Go home. You be here too much."

"She staying?" he asked, pointing to Shanna.

Shanna wasn't invited. But she said she was staying. And all during dinner them two made eyes at each other. Ain't talk to me, not once. So I had to listen to my mother and father get on my case about my last French test. I got a B minus. They put me on punishment for that.

"Here," Mookie said, handing Shanna's napkin to her after it fell off her lap to the floor.

"You gonna be my Prince Charming, huh?" she said, wiping grease off his mouth.

Mookie had this weird look in his eyes. "I'll be your Prince Charming, Robin Hood, Mac Daddy, Flunky, Fool. . . ."

"Oh, cut it out!" I said.

My mother told me to hush.

"Don't hate," Shanna said, moving her chair closer to Mookie. Taking her fork, piling it with mashed potatoes and gravy and feeding him like a baby.

My mother liked that. "Shanna. You can come by here anytime."

Mookie got a way with females. All he gotta do is walk into a room and they start doing stuff for him. Don't even know the boy and they offering to wash his clothes, clean his room, buy him stuff. His last girlfriend paid his cell phone bill for three months.

It ain't just that Mookie is a looker, with his jet-black curls and his honey-brown eyes, high cheeks, and long baby lashes. It's the way he was raised. The stuff women in this family taught him about how a boy treats a girl. Boys that open doors. Boys that compliment your hair and legs and smile. Boys that listen and touch your hand when they talking to you. Boys that know it ain't money that girls really want: it's time. And slow walks in the park, love notes, handwritten poems, and faithfulness. Boys who don't pull on you like they own you, but kiss your lips like they made of the sweetest chocolate in the world.

Mookie know all the secrets a girl keeps locked deep inside or stashed away in her diary. And he uses it to his advantage. I tried to tell Shanna that. She ain't listen, and before the night was done, she was letting him walk her home. Blushing when he said he wanted to meet her momma, if that was all right.

Before Mookie left the house, I pulled him aside. "She's nice. Got potential in this world. You mess with her, and I'm gonna—"

Mookie took my hand and kissed it. "Cousin-girl," he said, "that one I'm gonna treat right."

I almost threw up the garlic steak I ate for dinner. "What?"

"Something 'bout her," he said. "Something 'bout her makes a brother wanna do right."

I wanted to tell him that he just met her. Didn't even know her last name or how old she was. But it was right there in his eyes like a sign over the highway: MOOKIE IN LOVE.

The women in the family noticed it before the men. So come four Saturdays from the day them two met, all the women got together at our house to play spades. Momma figured it was time they talked about Mookie. Time to do something 'bout this girl he was with so much of the time.

"He brought her to my house," Aunt Lucinda said. "The boy ain't done that since he was ten years old," she said, laying down the king of clubs.

I took up for Mookie, which surprised me, too. "He's seventeen. Time he settled down, ain't it?"

Mookie's mom shook her head. "No," Aunt Lucinda said. "Not my baby. He too young to settle down."

"Too pretty, too," Momma said, putting down a three of spades and winning the hand. She led with the queen of hearts.

I was surprised at Momma, really. She was so nice to Shanna that first day at the house when she and Mookie met. Then the more she saw them two together, the meaner she got, and the more phone calls she started making to the aunts—saying there was something different 'bout this girl.

There are fifteen women and six girls in our family on my mother's side. All of 'em were there, including the newborn baby, Cara. It wasn't just that these women didn't want Mookie settling down with this girl. They didn't want Mookie settling down with any girl. They all figured that there were so many girls who didn't know how to be treated right by boys that Mookie ought not to be selfish by sticking to just one.

"We taught him right," said one of the aunts. "He the only boy I know who opens car doors."

"Carries your groceries and makes coffee just like you want," said another.

I went to the kitchen. Came back with a bowl of raspberry punch that I sat in the middle of the table. "Y'all talk like Mookie a angel. He treat girls good, but he dog some of 'em, too."

Everybody stopped talking and looked at me.

"He the only boy in the family for three generations," they all said at once.

I kicked off my shoes.

"Gonna make somebody a fine husband one
day," my aunt Grace said.

"Shanna say one day him and her gonna get married," I said.

Mookie's mother is a little thing, just five feet.
But when she stood up and came after me, it seem
like she was six feet tall. "Now let me tell you
something, missy!" she screamed. "That boy's too
young to settle down. And when he do, I'm gonna
do the picking!"

Three aunts raised their voices at once. "We!
We gonna do the picking."

"All of us," said my mother. "Since we all had a
hand in raising him."

The card party went on till midnight. We ain't
talk about the weather outside. (It was ninety-five
degrees and this was just late May.) We ain't talk
about the war the country was maybe getting into.
And we ain't talk about who was going to Mookie's
graduation next month. All we talked about the
whole time was Mookie and Shanna, and how to
break 'em up.

* * *

"Hey, cuz," Mookie said, laying a juicy, wet kiss on my cheek.

I wiped it off. "Save it for your girlfriend."

He went in the fridge and made hisself a sandwich. "That girl got my head spinning," he said, turning in circles. "Done made me tear up my datebook, change my e-mail address, and get a new cell number."

I tried to feel him out. "She just a girl, right? No biggie."

Mookie followed me onto the back porch. Started talking crazy. Telling me stuff I ain't wanna hear.

"It sounds stupid. But soon as I looked in her eyes, it happened."

"What . . . happened?"

"You know."

I wanted to make him say it. To spit it out in the air. "I don't know nothing," I said, throwing moldy bread to the birds.

Mookie stretched out one of his curls and twisted it around his finger. "I fell for that girl ASAP. *Bam!* Instantly."

My heart got all warm inside. "Naaah."

66

Mookie took hold of both my arms. "Cousin-girl, it was like in the movies. For real, you know. That night, I went home. Got my house in order. Ditched them other chicks."

"For real?"

"For real. Ain't telling my boys nothing like this. But . . . she got me going. You know?"

I felt sorry for Mookie. Here he was doing the right thing, finally being the boy my mother and the aunts really raised him to be, and they was gonna do their best to mess it up. Just so they could keep him to themselves.

I watched a blue jay eat crumbs off the porch railing. "Maybe you and Shanna shouldn't be 'round Momma and 'em so much."

Mookie stomped his feet when six more birds came to eat. "What?"

Women in our family stick together. So I wasn't gonna come right out and tell Mookie what was up. "I mean, Shanna's probably tired of being 'round all us, anyhow. You two ate here three days last week. Then y'all went to a play with your mother, and was at Aunt Sukkie's, Aunt Mildred's, Marie's, and Gionna's house, too. Seem like the girl would want to spend time with her side, sometimes."

Mookie thought awhile. "Maybe. It's just that I'm used to my side."

"Used to people waiting on you hand and foot. Giving you money and washing your drawers whenever you say."

He laughed, and I could see why Shanna fell so hard for him. Everything about him was perfect, even his cute little hands. "I ain't never giving up my family for no girl," he said, going back inside. "See you later. At dinner."

"Don't come here. I'm telling you."

He pressed his face to the screen, looking like a monster from TV. "We ain't coming here. Your family's coming to our place tonight. Everybody is."

I was scared to hear that. Especially since my mother ain't tell me nothing 'bout it. So, soon as Mookie left, I got on the phone. Called Shanna. The girl just as hardheaded as Mookie, though. She said she had to come, 'cause Mookie's momma invited her personally. Poor thing. She ain't know what Walker women could do when they put their mind to it.

"How come you ain't tell me dinner was over here?" I said to my mother just before we walked into Mookie's house.

She handed me the platter of smothered liver and bacon, and told my father not to forget the watermelon fruit salad in the car. Soon as he finished bringing in the rest of the food, though, they made him leave. Made all the men leave and eat in the den. And when Mookie asked why, the women all smiled. Said they had a surprise for him and Shanna.

Nothing special happened almost the whole time we was there. People ate. People drank. People farted and watched TV. Then just before we was all ready to leave, the aunts asked to see Shanna—alone. They took her to the bedroom. Told me I better not even try to come in. Shanna looked back at me and smiled. I think she thought something nice was gonna happen to her there. It didn't. She came out crying. When Mookie asked her what was wrong, she almost knocked his head off. "You got some girl pregnant?"

I stared at him. He stared at the aunts and me and my cousins. "What?"

Shanna ran out the door. My mother smiled. Her sisters almost busted out laughing. Mookie was too busy chasing Shanna to ask them why they lied on him. So I asked. Aunt Lucinda said it was for his own good. "To protect him from girls who got their own agendas."

"What?" I asked.

My mother scraped chicken bones into a plastic bag. "We know the kind of girl he needs."

My arms started shaking. "Mookie's almost a man. Y'all ain't got the right—"

Aunt Grace stood up and shut me down. "Girl! We protecting the family. Making sure the line stays pure . . . clean."

"What?" I said.

Aunt Lucinda said Mookie ain't have no business trying to date just one girl. That he needed to date around so they could see who was good enough for him.

"Five years from now he gonna be married," Momma said.

"And babies gonna be coming then."

Aunt Lucinda crossed her arms. "And we got the right to pick the girl who gonna give birth to the next boy in this family."

Me and Mookie are the oldest cousins, so there was no one left to take up for him but me.

"But he's just seventeen. Ain't thinking 'bout marriage . . . or babies."

Aunt Lucinda said she liked Shanna. But Shanna's side don't produce nothing but girl babies. "Them two get married and only girls coming. No way around it."

They crazy, I thought.

"That boy got our future inside him," Aunt Hattie whispered. "So we got the *right* to interfere. To make sure . . ."

I covered my ears. "I'm-a tell my father," I said, running to the door.

Aunt Lucinda blocked my way. "Gal . . ." she said, her fist in the air like a club.

I looked at my mother.

"Women raised Mookie," Momma said. "He ours. We know best."

I looked at my aunt's arm still high in the air. "You don't own Mookie. Anyhow, he better now than before."

Aunt Lucinda said I was too young to understand. "He ran around with trash before. But this one . . ."

"She nice," Momma said.

"She makes him crazy in the head," Aunt Luesta said.

"Got him to thinking that maybe she could be the one," another aunt said.

I opened my mouth, but I shouldn't have. "She could. Shanna could be his wife one day. She's nice like that."

They all came over to me. "She ain't never gonna be more than she is to him right now."

"An ex-girlfriend," Mookie's mother said.

"Some girl he thinks stole from his momma."

I looked at Aunt Lucinda. Asked her what she was talking about. She said it was in the plan. If Mookie makes up with Shanna tonight, she gonna tell him that they ain't want to hurt his feelings by telling him Shanna stole off her, so they just made up a lie to Shanna 'bout him, hoping that would be the end of her.

Aunt Lucinda smiled. "He ain't never gonna be with no girl that do his mother wrong."

Mookie and Shanna made up. But Aunt Lucinda was right. When she told him the lie 'bout Shanna, Mookie believed it. Called Shanna and they got to fighting. Shanna's momma called Mookie's momma and things got bigger and worse. When it was all done, the police was called in and a report was filed. And Mookie and Shanna was done . . . kinda. They both kept calling me, though. Talking to me 'bout the other. I couldn't tell Mookie what I knew. Couldn't tell Shanna how strange our family was. So for two months them two didn't see each other. Mookie ain't date nobody else, though. He came over to our place. Looked all pitiful. And just when he talked hisself into calling Shanna, one of the aunts got him to go someplace with her. She filled his head with all kind of stuff. And for another month, he was finished with Shanna again. Then one day, I just made up my mind. I was gonna get them back together. So I did.

"Walk me to the store, Mookie," I said, grabbing him by the arm.

When we got outside, he pushed me to the left side so he could walk on the traffic side. I asked him when was the last time he saw Shanna. He ain't answer. I told him I had a stop to make. At a friend's. When we got there, the girl wasn't home. I knew that from the start. But she was Shanna's cousin, and Shanna was spending the weekend there, so I asked for her. Shanna almost died when she saw Mookie.

"What you want?" she said, walking out the room.

Mookie just stared at her like she was the most beautiful girl in the world.

"You know Shanna ain't no thief," I told Mookie. Then I looked at Shanna. "And you know Mookie don't cheat. Well, he used to. But never on you."

I could tell Mookie wanted to kiss her. That she wanted him to hold her and make everything all right.

"Mookie, your momma's a liar," I said. "Mine too." I sat on the couch. "All of 'em lying, just to keep you to themselves."

Mookie wasn't listening, really. He was talking to Shanna. Saying he was sorry he ain't believe her. Apologizing for his mother.

Shanna was crying, saying she knew deep down inside that he would never cheat on her.

They kissed. They kissed the way I want a boy to kiss me one day. Kissed like they loved each other for always—like nothing and nobody was ever gonna break 'em up again.

"Don't tell Aunt Lucinda or Momma," I said to Mookie. "Or they will break y'all up again. For good."

Shanna said she didn't understand why they

hated her so much. I told 'em both what Aunt Lucinda told me.

"I ain't ready for babies," Mookie said, rubbing Shanna's neck.

"I'm only seventeen," she said. "I'm going to college next year."

"It don't matter what you two want. Walker women want baby boys. Plenty of 'em. They been planning for 'em since Mookie's been born," I said. "And they think they got the right to pick the momma, too."

Shanna said the aunts were right. Her side don't give birth to nothing but girls.

Mookie sucked on her pretty pink lips. "I like girls."

I told him we needed a plan if him and Shanna wanted to stay together.

Mookie said he would keep doing for the aunts like he always did. Help carry their groceries. Shovel their snow and hold their umbrellas when it rained. Come to dinner and listen to 'em talk about the good old days. "I won't mention Shanna's name, ever."

Shanna didn't like that.

"Won't bring her around my mother, or yours."

"Naw," I said. "They know you like girls. If they don't see one around you, they gonna figure you creeping back here to Shanna."

Mookie walked over to the window. "Forget it. I'm moving out, then. Gonna live with my dad across town."

I told him that wouldn't work. They would just call him all the time. Beg him to come over to do this and that.

We spent the whole next hour trying to come up with something. Then just when we was gonna give up, Shanna came up with the perfect plan. "Seems to me they just want some boys in the family. Baby boys they can raise up any way they like."

"Duh!" me and Mookie said.

"Then they should adopt one. Or get one from foster care. Or open a day-care center," Shanna said.

I shook my head. "No. The baby's gotta have Walker blood."

Shanna kept talking. Saying that maybe for now the aunts wouldn't be so picky. "They'd be so busy with the baby, they wouldn't have time to fuss over Mookie."

I told Shanna her idea wouldn't work. My mother and aunts wouldn't adopt nobody.

"Would they babysit, then? I mean, take care of a little newborn baby boy?" She headed upstairs and came back down with a tiny, little baby wrapped in a yellow blanket.

Mookie's eyes got big. "That ain't mine," he said, looking at me.

Shanna said it was her cousin's boyfriend's sister's kid. He was here 'cause they didn't have a steady babysitter to care for it. "Every week it's someplace else. He's three months old and keeps a cold."

"All them strangers and germs," I said, sniffing his sweetness.

Mookie got on the phone. Called my mother and asked how come she ain't invite him to dinner lately. She asked him what he wanted to eat. Before he hung up, he told her she should invite the aunts over too. "Been a while since we all been together."

All the aunts came. They brought chips and cakes and pies, stewed chicken, barbecued chicken, chicken salad, and chicken on a stick. They made potato salad, pretzel salad, spinach dips, sauces, seasonings, and more salads. There was too much food and too many aunts. By the time we finished eating, couldn't nobody hardly walk or talk.

That's when Mookie said he had to make a run. When he came back, he had the baby in his arms.

"Oh, my goodness!" his mother said.

"It's not mine, Mom," he said, heading her way, laying the baby in her lap.

All the aunts came to look, to touch and count toes and fingers. Mookie told 'em he was babysitting. Helping out a friend of a friend. He said it was terrible, the way the baby ain't have a permanent babysitter. His mother said the baby had on too much clothing. My mother asked about the rash over his left eye. Aunt Grace wondered who was taking care of the child. "'Cause they doing a poor job, I'll tell you that."

By the time the party was over, all the aunts had agreed that they could do a better job raising the boy than the people doing it now.

"Sure could," Mookie said, putting the blanket back on the baby.

Then he asked them if they wanted him to ask the mother if it would be okay for them to babysit. The nine sisters said it all at once: "Oh, my. Yes!"

Mookie and Shanna been together for six whole months now. His mother never asks who he's going out with. The aunts don't care much if he comes by once a week or not. They always at his house, though—wiping green peas off the baby's chin, patting his back, or bouncing him on their laps. "Ain't he the cutest thing," they say.

"I thought I was the cutest thing," Mookie said the other day.

"You *was*," my mother said, and laughed, tucking her nose deep in the baby's neck and sniffing the lavender bath lotion on his skin.

Mookie and me walked out the front door and around the corner. "See you later, cuz," he said, hugging me.

"Later," I said, heading for the store, watching him and Shanna walk over to the park holding hands and laughing.

Don't Be Disrespecting Me

THE GIRLS LIKED Erin, but not his name. So they called him E. He liked it, especially when Ona called him that.

E's boys teased him about Ona. She lived in the suburbs and couldn't even get phone calls from boys. But she liked E, even though he came from the part of town that everybody called Death Row.

"Ona think she better than us," E's boy Noodles said. They were at E's house, lying on his bed—a pile of thin woolly blankets on the floor.

E thought about Ona's pretty smile and her apple-butter brown skin. "She's all right," he said.

"Invite her to your *crib* then."

"One day," E said, rubbing his gloved hands together.

Noodles stood up and looked through the thick, clear plastic covering E's bedroom window. "Man, when your momma gonna get the heat cut back on?"

Even with the plastic, E could see frost on the windows and his breath sometimes when he breathed out. "You got heat?"

"Well, we . . ."

"Then shut up."

For a long time, they talked about girls. Then E said they should go to the mall. "It's warm there."

"They got girls there, too," Noodles said. "And girls always got some dough."

On the bus, Noodles talked about how he was gonna get some girl to buy him pizza. "And hot chocolate, too." He wasn't lying. E knew that. He once saw Noodles talk a girl into paying his way to a $60 rap concert. Saw him get girls in school to lend him bus money, even though the school already gives every student a bus pass.

"Don't be hustling girls around me," E said, getting off the bus and heading for the mall.

Noodles shook his head. "I was born broke, but that don't mean I have to stay broke, especially when so many girls got so much money."

E ignored Noodles. He rubbed his big toe

against the hole in his sneaker, then walked over to the pharmacy and put in a job application. A half hour later, E saw Noodles with his arms hanging over some girl's shoulder. E stood nearby while Noodles took her over to a cold concrete seat, sat her down, and talked . . . till she took him to the food court and bought him two slices of pizza and a supersize drink. Noodles came back and told E he shoulda come, too. "She had long dollars. Shoot. I coulda got me a shirt out the deal if I wanted."

E's stomach was growling. He hardly ever ate at the mall 'cause he didn't ever have the money. "Let's go," he said. Then he told Noodles how he put in three job applications while Noodles was gone.

Noodles pulled out five bucks. "Here," he said, stuffing the money in E's pocket. "She went to the ATM machine. I told her I'd pay her back, when I could."

E shook his head. Told himself to give the money back, but he didn't. He bought a piece of pizza and a drink, then listened to Noodles say how he was gonna get that girl to buy him some new sneakers and take him out a few times.

On the bus ride home, E wondered what Ona and her family did on weekends. On Mondays, she always seemed to have on some new outfit or a new piece of jewelry. E always looked the same: jeans, run-over sneakers, and a coat with sleeves much too short.

"That's how it is when you got eight brothers and sisters," he once told a boy after he'd cracked on the hole in his shirt. Two days later, E stole some jeans off a clothesline in the backyard near his school. Now every year before school started, he stole one pair of jeans. Even so, kids still teased him about his clothes. But not Ona. She never seemed to notice. E never told his boys, but he dreamed about that girl at night. The dreams always ended the same, too—with Ona and him kissing and holding each other tight.

Ona knew better than to be making eyes at a boy like E.

"Dirt poor," her friends called him behind his back.

But Ona liked him anyway. Figured you could always make a nice person look like something. But a no-class knucklehead like Noodles is gonna be just that, no matter how much you dress him up, she thought.

Over the weekend, she finally did what she'd been wanting to do. She got her sister Brenda to drive her past E's house. She'd never seen anything like it. "A shack," Brenda called it. Her boyfriend said the fire marshal should condemn the whole block, then strike a match and keep on walking.

"See?" Brenda said. "You never know who you're gonna sit next to when you go to a public school."

Brenda was in her second year of college. She'd gone to private school all her life. So had their older brother, Melvin. By the time Ona came along, her parents had softened. They told her she could go to high school wherever she liked, as long as the school had a good reputation and a scholars' track for really smart kids.

E wasn't in the scholars' program. But he and Ona still had a few classes together: art, music, and civics. Since their last names started with the same initial (hers was Bleton, his Boven), they always ended up sitting next to each other. She liked him right away. When she slipped and fell the first day of class, he was the only one who didn't laugh.

She noticed him at lunch. Not eating or drinking. Stuck over in the corner reading, unless

Noodlehead Noodles was messing with him. She saw his outdated clothes and high-water pants, his perfect teeth and chestnut-brown skin.

"Loser," her friends had said, when she'd first said she liked him.

"He's cute," she'd told them.

Maria whispered, but she'd meant for E to hear. "He lives on Death Row. Gonna be on Death Row for real one day, too."

Every night Ona took out E's picture—the one she'd taken from his notebook when he wasn't looking—and kissed him good night. "Ask me to the homecoming dance," she'd say to the picture. "Ask me, and just watch if I don't say yes."

In civics, E leaned over and asked Ona if she had a pencil. She gave him one that her dad had bought from a New York City bookstore for $8. "Keep it," she said, twisting her hair.

E sniffed. Ona smelled good, like always. He touched the tip of her soft brown hair and wondered what it would be like to dance with her. Slow dance. In a nice place, not in the basement of the school where the kids stank with sweat and danced like they were already in bed.

Ona tried to be cool. To act like she wasn't

about to jump out of her skin 'cause E was so close to her. But she couldn't help it. Her fingers were shaking. Her eyes blinked more than they should. "I . . ." Ona couldn't get the words out. "I . . ." She promised herself all the way to school she was just gonna come out and say she liked him. And that she wanted him to call her sometimes, even if her dad didn't want boys calling the house. "I . . ." she said again. But it was too late. The bell rang.

Noodles almost knocked Ona down trying to get to E. E pushed Noodles so hard his books fell on the floor. "Man. Ain't you got no manners?" he said. "I'm with somebody."

Noodles wanted to fight E right then and there. He didn't like being embarrassed. But he kept his hands at his side 'cause E was his boy. He would let him slide, this time, he thought.

Ona was so happy. *He likes me,* she thought. Then she brought up the homecoming dance. "You going?"

E bit down on his lip and watched Noodles slink away. "Naw. I don't do stuff like that."

Ona waved to her friend Maria. A few minutes later she was sorry, though, 'cause right away Maria asked Ona whom she was going to the dance with. Before Ona answered, Maria turned to E. "For sure you're not going with him. Unless you got a dress that matches holey jeans and dirty sneakers."

Ona grabbed a hunk of her friend's arm and pinched.

"Ouch!"

Ona's eyes dared her friend to say a word, then she and E headed for art class in silence. When the teacher turned off the lights to show them a film, Ona apologized to E. He played it off. Said he'd already forgotten about her bigmouthed friend. "Anyhow, I could go to the dance if I wanted."

Ona felt sorry for him.

"You going?" E asked her.

She moved her desk closer to his. "You wanna take me?"

E didn't say a word at first. But his head was full of excuses. *I ain't got no clothes, no ride, no money for the dance tickets.* But when he spoke, the word "Yes," came out strong and clear, like it had been sitting on his tongue for years, just waiting to give Ona whatever she wanted.

Ona's head turned around so fast she heard her neck bones crack. "Okay. What color are you going to wear?"

E couldn't open his mouth. All he kept thinking was how stupid he was for asking Ona to go to the dance when he knew his mother didn't have any money to get new clothes, and he didn't have a job.

Noodles popped E upside the head when E told him what he'd done. E sat in his bedroom window. Pushed at the puffed-out plastic filled with wind. "Maybe I can still find a job or something."

Noodles asked E how many applications he'd put in over the last six months.

"Thirty."

"Well, ain't you figured it out yet? They don't want you," Noodles said.

E looked scared. Embarrassed, too. "The jitney station might give me a few dollars for cleaning up."

Noodles came over to E. Pulled out a chocolate bar. "Only one thing to do," he said, breaking the candy in two. "Steal it."

E was quiet for a long while. "Steal what?"

"Whatever you need. Clothes. Shoes. Socks."

E watched the crap game going on across the street.

"Steal the money, or steal the clothes," Noodles said. "Shoot. I need me some clothes, too."

E's sisters came into the room and started digging through a tall brown box in which they kept their clothes. "I need to put another shirt on. It's cold in here," six-year-old Erie said.

E stared at the gloves on her hands. Looked at his sister in a torn jacket, and heard Noodles's words loud and clear. "Steal it." So that's what he did.

Noodles just wanted to go to a store, try on some clothes, and walk out. E wanted the money. Said his sisters needed stuff, too. And his mother needed help with the bills.

"What you planning to do? Rob a bank?" Noodles laughed.

E smiled.

"A bank. For real? Cool," Noodles said.

"Get a brain, Noodles."

"We could rip off teachers. Take the money right out their purses," Noodles said.

E liked that idea but turned it down. He didn't want to be kicked out of school if they got caught. Then he thought about something Ona had said. People around her way rarely locked their doors and windows. He was telling her about his neighborhood with women walking the street in hot-pink furs and no underwear. She was talking about hers, where people kept big dollars in upstairs drawers for hard times that never seemed to come.

Later that night, E and Noodles figured out just when and how they'd get the money. Come midnight, E put Noodles out of his house. Said he was going to bed. He couldn't sleep, though. His brothers kept coughing and snotting. "I shoulda stepped up to the plate a long time ago," he said to himself. "Shoulda been a man long before now."

They noticed it right away: the houses in Green Oak Park looked like small apartment buildings. People had smoking chimneys and pretty green shrubs, even though it was January and frost covered everything.

Nobody was outside and not too many houses had cars out front. So they walked from house to house, peeking inside, since people didn't have their shades down or their curtains closed.

"They live right out in the open," Noodles said. "You do something like that on Death Row, you gonna get shot just for being stupid."

E liked the beige-and-white house with the

statue out front. It had a curved brick walkway and a welcome sign out front with the family's name on it. He walked around back. The rose-colored kitchen was empty. He tried the doorknob. No problem. "People here don't lock doors, just like Ona said."

Noodles went in first. Said if somebody answered, he'd just act like he was in the wrong house. But nobody was home. So they ran upstairs. Dug in the drawers. Made up a rap song when they found $600 in the drawer in the master bedroom. They snatched cupcakes and cinnamon rolls on the way out. Then walked, like nothing was up, all the way out of the neighborhood.

E gave Noodles half the money. Said he wasn't doing this anymore. But it felt good when he told Ona that he'd paid for the tickets. It felt good wearing new jeans and sneakers and having kids fuss over him. But the money ran out before he gave his mother any. So two weeks later when Noodles said they should do it again, E was game.

"Friday's our lucky day," Noodles said. "So let's do it again on Friday."

Noodles picked the house this time. They walked in, sat on the furniture, and even watched a little TV. E looked around the room, at the shiny white piano and the fluffy cream-colored furniture. "How some people end up with all the money in the world, and other folks end up poor as dirt? Like us."

Noodles flipped from channel to channel. "That's why God gave people a bad gene. So they got the guts to even this money thing out and get some of what other folks got too much of."

It made sense, E thought. So he picked up a clear candy dish with pink swans for handles and took it with him when he left. "For Momma," he said.

Ona knew that more girls would like E if they saw what she saw in him. But she didn't know that it would happen so fast. Since he dressed better, the girls spoke to him more, looked at him longer. Ona asked E how he dressed so fly all of a sudden. He lied. Said his mother finally got herself a decent man to take care of their family. She believed him. Didn't see anything different in him. He still came to class. Did all his homework. Looked at her like he would die without her. He was still E. So she invited him to her house. "'Cause my father won't let me go to the dance with anyone he hasn't met."

She told him that her dad would pick him up. E said he'd take the bus over. It was weird, showing up at her place. All the houses in that neighborhood were the same inside, so he knew where every room in her house was without even asking.

"You seem like a nice boy," Ona's mother said, handing him a plate piled with liver and fried onions, a baked potato, and asparagus spears.

Her dad stared at him. Said he looked familiar. "Ever been around here before?" he asked, playing with his gold pinky ring with a black diamond chip on it.

"No, sir. I ain't never been around here," E said.

Ona's mom corrected his English. Her dad frowned and asked E to take his elbows off the table.

Ona was so embarrassed. Her father was mean to E. He didn't like boys calling her or coming to their house. And he especially didn't like boys from Death Row. "When boys from that part of town are born, they don't give 'em a birth certificate," he told her once. "They tattoo a prison number on their butts."

Ona wanted to scream when he'd said that. To tell him that E wasn't like that. But she saw the clothes. Heard kids say he was selling weed. Wondered what he was up to.

E knew before he left that Ona's father wouldn't let him take her to the dance. He tried to be nice. To look up from his plate when they spoke to him, but he couldn't after a while. And even though he had on new sneakers and an outfit that cost almost a hundred and fifty bucks, he felt like a bum. Ona's father made sure of that.

"Man, you went all outta your way for that chick, and her dad treated you like that?" Noodles said, soon as E got back home.

E tried to play it off. But Noodles kept saying that E had to get Ona's dad back for disrespecting him.

"It don't matter," E said, taking off his jacket. Sweating from the heat.

"Yes it *do* matter," Noodles said, throwing punches in the air. "It matters anytime somebody treats you less than what you is."

E's mouth tasted sour. He opened the window and spit. The wind and snow flurries turned his face as cold and hard as the ice on the window ledge.

"Man, do something," he said. "Don't be no punk."

E told Noodles to go home.

"Don't worry. I'll fix her dad for you, and jack her up too," Noodles said.

E's fist slammed into Noodle's chest, shoulder, and right cheek. Noodles ducked and swung. E's mother broke up the fight. The next day, Noodles was at E's house, looking for something to eat— like usual.

Ona tried to tell him nicely. But there's no way to tell a boy three days before the second-biggest dance of the year that you can't go with him. So ultimately she just came right out with it. She didn't look E in the eyes, though. She stared down at a piece of paper on the hallway floor. Grabbed his hand and said that maybe she could meet him there anyhow. "My father doesn't have to know," she said, finally looking into his eyes.

E's mother didn't ask any questions. She was glad to have the heat, new clothes for the little ones, and some extra change in her pocket. She was *glad* to ask the neighbors to come over and see how good E looked in a suit. "People go to these kinds of dances on a bus?" she asked when he headed out the door. "You sure?"

E didn't care if he had to walk. He was going to the dance. Going with Ona. Dressed up in new fancy clothes for the first time since his sixth-grade graduation.

When he stepped on the bus, he smiled. He could see people staring. Whispering. Noticing the boy in the sharp suit, carrying his coat on his arm. "People gonna see what I got on," he told his mother when she said he'd better wear that coat. "Even if I freeze, they gonna get a good look at me."

When he got to the school, people clapped. They whistled. They came up to him and touched his clothes and eyed his rings and asked if his mother hit the lottery. It felt good, being popular. Having girls wink and smile and press close to you, just because, E thought.

"No, I don't wanna dance," he said to Maria. "I'm looking for Ona. You see her?"

Maria waved her little finger for him to come closer. "She can't come," she said, blowing in his ear. "They got robbed." She told him that Ona's bedroom got trashed the worst. "Cuss words were smeared on her walls in black Magic Marker.

Her clothes were cut up and her stuffed animals were shoved in the toilet."

E looked up just when Noodles walked in the room in a powder-blue sweater, black pants, matching black gator shoes, and a gold pinky ring with a black-chip diamond in the middle.

E ran over to him. "What you think you doing, man?"

Noodles smiled. "I told you. Don't be disrespecting me," he said, rubbing the ring and walking away. Then, turning back around and leaning against the wall, Noodles talked. His words jumped high over the loud music, then snuck down low when the sax, the drums, and the singing smoothed out, and then disappeared till the next CD took over. "It was nice being there all by myself. Kicking it with her dad's gin and brew and her mother's fancy wineglasses."

E shook his head. Noodles kept talking.

"I smashed the grandfather clock first. Pow!" he said, closing one eye and firing an invisible gun.

E felt sick.

"Glass flies like tiny airplanes, you know?" Noodles looked at the ceiling like he could see

97

planes overhead. "I mean, that stuff was in the yard, the kitchen, the family room—everywhere!"

E blinked and rubbed his eyes like he was see- ing somebody else standing in front of him, not Noodles.

"Then I took my boots and spread peanut butter on the bottoms and walked on that dude's white rugs, and his white couch, and his pretty white bedspreads. That one was for you," Noodles said.

E hated Ona's dad, but he clocked Noodles in the chest anyhow. It was dark and the teachers were busy complimenting kids on their clothes and talking to each other, so they didn't notice.

Noodles always could take a hit, so he kept talking. Telling E how he poured hot syrup on Ona's bedroom furniture and jerked her curtains off the rods and stuffed 'em into sinks that he filled up with water.

E watched the girls in their low-cut gowns laugh and shake and smile. "Ona," he said.

"Man, forget her," Noodles told him. "She home pulling glass out her bed and washing pee off the walls."

E wanted a knife or a gun. *I should cut him,* he thought. *Or shoot him right in his big mouth.*

Noodles knew when to stay clear of E, so he took off. He ran over to a girl and pulled her onto the dance floor even though she didn't wanna go.

"It won't matter," E said. *Ona's never gonna be mine nohow,* he thought. So he left Noodles alone.

When the police showed up, Noodles started running before the cops even said who they were looking for. They bent his arms way behind his back and elbowed him when he spit and cussed at them.

E didn't move. He sipped sparkling pink punch. Broke open a piece of chocolate and sucked the cherry out. He listened for Noodles to yell his name. He didn't even give the police a hard time when they came for him.

"I told you, don't be disrespecting me. Not for no stinking girl," Noodles said to E. Then he laughed.

E didn't ask the cop why he was hauling him off to jail. And he didn't say one word to Noodles on the long ride, either. He closed his eyes and imagined himself and Ona dancing—holding tight to each other. Ignoring all those people who wondered what she ever saw in him.

I Like White Boys

"I LIKE WHITE BOYS," I tell my friend Winter when she sits down in the seat next to me.

"Who doesn't know that?" she says, rolling her eyes, then sticking two fingers in her mouth and pretending to throw up.

I slide my chair closer to hers. "I especially like Johnny," I say, looking over at him.

Winter pats her own cheeks. "I only like boys that look like me. Brown. Black. Sweet as cho-co-lat."

I ignore Winter and take another long look at Johnny, leaning on the wall, holding hands with his girlfriend, Wendy. Wendy's got strawberry-blond hair, blue eyes, and a big chest. Boys at this school like girls like that. And there are more Wendys here than girls like me and Winter.

"He's so cute," I say, closing my eyes and pretending it's me he's holding.

Winter pokes me in the side with her elbow. "Forget it. You ain't his type."

I get on Winter's case about the way she speaks. "Don't say *ain't*."

"*Ain't* ain't a bad word," Winter says. "Anyhow, that's how we talk in the ghetto. Right?"

Me and Winter both come from the other side of town. *Ghetto girls*, the kids around here call us sometimes behind our backs. They know we don't really belong. That we're on scholarship at this private school, just like most of the other black and Hispanic kids that go here.

I lower my voice so Johnny can't hear when he takes his seat next to me. "I'm just saying. You know how to speak *good* English."

Winter shakes her head and tells me that "*Black English*" is *good* English. "But maybe it ain't good enough for a girl like you. A black girl who only likes white boys."

I don't get mad when she says that, because it's true. Ever since I was five, I've liked boys that look like Johnny better than the ones that look like me. I never told anyone, though—until I met Winter.

I didn't tell her either, not exactly. She figured it out. Said all she ever heard me say is how cute the blue-eyed boys were. Or the ones with blond hair and extra-white skin. "What about the brothers?" she asked.

"What about 'em?" I said. Then I told her that when I was little I'd kiss the blond-haired boys right on the lips when they came on TV. Winter talked bad about me after that. But she never stopped being my friend.

Winter points to Johnny. "How can you like him?" she says louder than she should. "He's got donkey ears." She frowns. "Skin like rice paper. And eyes that turn red as blood when you take pictures of 'em." She reaches around me and taps him on the shoulder. "Hey, Vampire Boy. You. . . .You!" she says, snapping her fingers like he's a waiter taking too long to bring her food.

Johnny opens his mouth to say something to her, then shakes his head.

"You do your homework?" he asks me.

My smile is extra big. "Yeah. You?"

"Most of it," he says. Then Wendy asks him something, and it's like he was never talking to me in the first place.

When Mr. G walks into the room, he points to me, Johnny, and Winter, and says we're in group one. He wants the class to come up with a new ending for the story we've been reading for a month. "Come up with something creative. Unique," he says.

I sit as close as I can to Johnny. I check out his long platinum hair and sea-green eyes. I think about us being married one day, and having real pretty babies.

"High-yella babies, that's what I want," I told Winter once.

She looked at my arms and face, which are exactly the same color as hers: raisin-black without the wrinkles. "High yella's fine, but this is better," she said, rubbing her arm.

I didn't tell her, but I want my babies to be pretty. To have hair you don't have to relax, and skin that burns in the sun. All of my cousins are like that. Then there's me and my sister—Cocoa Puffs— that's what kids in the family call us when the grown-ups aren't around. I don't like that.

Winter pulls out a pen and pencil and tells Johnny to move his chair outta her way. "I'm in charge," she says, taking over our group.

Johnny ignores her, then hands me a note to give to a girl who will give it to Wendy.

"See?" Winter says. "He's not thinking about you." She turns to him and snaps her fingers. "You want to be in this group, or what?"

"Be nice," I whisper. Then I move my chair closer to his.

For the rest of the period, Winter sticks it to Johnny. She shuts him down when he tries to talk. She suggests that a black girl should steal the boy in our story from his white girlfriend, then waits for Johnny to say something different. He keeps quiet. Then Winter asks him what kind of girls he likes. His cheeks turn pink, and he starts picking at his ears. "I don't know. Somebody pretty, I guess. With hair down to here," he says, poking his ribs.

My fingers go to the short tight curls on my head. They don't even reach down to my eyebrows.

Winter likes to make people squirm. "You know anything about black girls, Johnny?"

"What?" he says, looking back at Wendy.

Winter won't leave him be. "You ever date one? A black girl, I mean. Ever had one in your house?"

I ask Winter if she ever had a white person over to her house.

"Yep," she says. "The mailman. The insurance man. The police."

I keep quiet and wonder why I even hang with her. But I know why. The other black kids can't stand me.

Mr. G yells over the first bell. "Five more minutes. Wrap it up, people."

Johnny finally answers Winter's question. "No. I never dated a black girl."

Winter goes into her purse, then smears a little grease on her ashy knees. "Ever have one in your house?"

He pulls at the long white strands on his arm. "Ever have what in my house?"

"A black girl. One of us," she says, pointing from me to her.

He raises his hand. "Mr. G, when did you say we had to be finished?"

"In three, two, one. Pencils down."

Johnny looks like he's glad class is over, even if we're gonna get in trouble for not completing the assignment. But when Winter tells Mr. G we didn't get that far, he cuts us a break. Says we can hand it in by the end of the day.

"Guess we have to lunch together," Winter says, packing up to leave.

Johnny looks sick when he hears that. "Not me," he says, reaching for Wendy's hand and walking out the door.

Winter and I go sit at the table at the back of the lunchroom where most of the black ninth-graders sit. When kids wanna be smart, they call it Little Africa. That's why I hardly ever sit there. That's one reason why the black and Hispanic kids call me a snob. But it's the third Friday of the month, the day Winter gets her way and we sit where she wants. So here I am.

"Melvin, you know you need your hair braided. I can start it now, finish up later," Winter says, sitting down.

Melvin digs in his back pocket for a comb. "Er'ka. Wanna help?" he says, talking to me.

"My name isn't Er'ka," I yell. "It's Erika. E-r-i-k-a," I say, thinking about how much I hate the way black boys say my name.

Winter laughs.

Melvin puts away the comb. "It's Erika. So say it the right way—the *white* way," he says, looking me up and down. He sucks his front teeth with his tongue like he's trying to get stuck food out. "You looking for the white kids? They're over there," he says, pointing around the cafeteria.

Winter tells him to chill. I complain about her agreeing to do his hair. She says I shoulda known they wouldn't comb hair in the cafeteria. "At least not in *this* school."

In a few minutes our table is full of kids. All black. All loud. Louder than anyone else in the lunchroom. I am so embarrassed. All the other kids are looking over their shoulders. Rolling their eyes. Wondering, I bet, why we can't act right. *Act white*, I hear Melvin's voice say in my head.

I grab Winter's lunch bag and head for another table. "Let's go," I say.

Melvin asks her why she puts up with me. "'Cause you're her only friend, you know." His lips curl and his words shrink like cheap bacon. "Only *black* one, anyhow."

Winter and I spend the rest of our lunch period working on the paper. When lunch is almost over, in walks Johnny. Winter makes sure he knows his name's not going on it now. It takes ten minutes for me to make them stop fighting. It's not Johnny's fault, though. The only reason Winter is so hard on him is because she knows how much I like him.

"Chet Richards likes you. And he's our color," she's said to me before. But do I only get to like boys that look like me? Or can I be like girls who look like Wendy, and get to pick any boy I want?

Johnny's tired of Winter, I guess. "Forget it," he says to her. "Don't put my name on the paper. I don't care."

I hand the paper to Johnny and let him read it.

Winter leans over the table and starts poking it. "I think the black girl in the story should be different."

Johnny moves his lips while he reads. "She's all right."

Winter looks at me. "See, I told you we need to spice her up." Her eyes turn Johnny's way. "For that girl to take Joey away from his girlfriend, she can't just be all right. She's gotta be slamming."

I finger my short, hard curls and wonder what it would be like to kiss Johnny on his tiny, pink lips. Right then, Melvin walks up to our table. He looks at me, then Johnny. "Got yourself a black girl, huh, Johnny?"

I roll my eyes. Johnny turns red. Winter laughs.

"Er'ka and you go together now?" he asks.

"Erika!" I say.

Johnny tells Melvin to mind his own business.

Melvin laughs, then tells Johnny that he should dump Wendy. "'Cause with Er'ka, you get two for one. A black girl on the outside, and a Wendy-white girl on the inside." He walks away.

When I stand up, seventeen Oreo cookies come after me like flat black-and-white hockey pucks. Bouncing off my tailbone. Knocking into the side of my head and smacking my shoulder and cheeks. Winter ducks, but gets hit upside the head anyhow.

"Cut it out!" Johnny shouts.

"Cut it out!" a kid at the table repeats.

Johnny asks me why they act like that.

"Like what?" Winter says, brushing crumbs out my hair.

"Forget it," he says, brushing off his shirt, then walking out the room when more kids from table nine head our way.

"That's the way the cookie crumbles," I hear one of 'em say when they pass by.

Winter speaks up then. Says she's gonna jack up the person who hit her with the cookie. The kids keep quiet and keep moving, because nobody messes with Winter. She is almost six feet tall, runs track, and fights like a boy. In sixth grade she beat the mess out of Gerald Manson for trying to touch her butt. In seventh grade she beat me up. She came up to me after school with her fist tight and her mouth running, and punched me in the face for telling the teacher she was cheating off my paper. I never told that she hit me, so she didn't get suspended like she should have. But the English teacher gave her an E for cheating and made her come to me for tutoring. "Since you think Erika is so smart, let's have her tutor you three days a week after school," she said. That's how we became friends. How I started telling her things I don't tell anybody else.

At the end of sixth period, Johnny comes up to me and says maybe he and I could finish the paper during study hall. I have him all to myself for a few minutes. But it's all over when Wendy walks over to him and says, "Let's go."

Johnny clears his throat when he tells her that he and I have to go finish up this paper. Wendy says something in his ear. Johnny looks down at his feet when he tells me he'll meet me in study hall. But before I take ten good steps, he's saying for me to just write what I want and put his name on it. Wendy's got him over by the lockers now. Grinning in his face. Playing with the keys bunched in his back pocket.

I don't like it, but I head for study hall all by myself. The place is packed, so I end up with a seat right next to Chet Richards, the boy Winter thinks is perfect for me. I smile at him, because he's smiling at me, not because I like him or anything.

Finally, I sit down and write. "*I like you,*" the white boy says to the black girl in my story. "*I like your big brown lips and the stuff you do with your hair.*"

Chet Richards interrupts me. "Hey, Erika?"

I don't even look his way. "Hi."

He keeps talking. Asking me about homework. Telling me about a new movie that's out. Making it hard for me to concentrate. I tell him that, too.

"*You know I like you too,*" the black girl tells the white boy on paper.

Chet drops his pen.

"Here!" I hand it to him.

"Thanks," he says, asking me if I'm going to the school carnival next week. Most kids go in couples.

I stare at him awhile so he knows not to say one more word to me. That's when I notice the way he looks at me. Dreamy-eyed. Kinda like I look at Johnny. "No," I say. "I'm not going."

Chet is a nice-looking boy. Long brown locs, medium-build with a beginner's mustache. But he's not my type. And ten minutes later he's at it again. Telling me how pretty my hair looks. My fingers roll over my curls. I want to tell him my hair is not like Wendy's or long like Johnny likes, but "Thanks," comes out instead.

After study hall, I head for my locker. The other black kids bump into me every chance they get. That's 'cause Winter isn't around. By the time I get to my locker, my arms hurt. But I don't care, 'cause soon as I get there, I see Johnny. He's by himself. And for twenty whole minutes he talks to me. Puts his name on the paper and even tells me to call him tonight if Winter tries to take it off.

Johnny reminds me of my cousin—his father is black and Jewish, and his mother is Swedish. He was the first boy I ever liked. The only boy who ever said I was beautiful.

"You can't marry your cousin," my mother said when I was five and I told her I was gonna marry him one day.

But I can marry Johnny, I think. And just when I go

to ask him to the carnival, Wendy pops up. Two minutes later, Johnny is gone, walking up the hall, holding her hand and not thinking about me at all.

Johnny doesn't like me. Winter tells me that all the time. But I keep thinking maybe, *maybe*, one day he will. I drop the paper off on Mr. G's desk before I head out.

When I get to the bus stop, Chet Richards walks up behind me. Covers my eyes and asks me to guess who it is. I know without looking, by the cologne he wears.

I tell him not to be so juvenile. He asks if he can wait for the bus with me. He lives three blocks from the school, so he doesn't get bused like most black kids.

"Yeah," I say, letting him take my book bag. "Thanks." I watch Johnny and Wendy pass by.

Chet is funny and smart. And even though the bus is late, he waits with me. He asks me about my family and neighborhood. Tells me what his parents do for a living and how they will all go to Greece this summer for a whole month. *You better hold on to him*, Winter would say. *He's got money.*

Chet gets real close and asks me again if I want to go to the carnival. For a minute, I think about saying yes. I mean, it's not like Johnny's *ever* gonna ask me out. But then this other boy walks by, bouncing on his toes—his long, blond hair swinging.

"Hey," I say, running after him. Forgetting all about Chet.

Jacobs's Rules

MR. JACOBS WAS getting mad. But that didn't stop us from talking. "Settle down!" he yelled again.

The boys did quiet down a bit. The big-mouthed girls kept right on yakking.

"Do you understand English?" Jacobs said, smacking his hands like cymbals, right in Marimba's face.

"Whatever," Marimba said, turning her back to him.

Jacobs picked up an algebra book and dropped it on the floor. "Okay, girls. Out of my room—now!"

Us boys really started talking then. Telling the girls to quiet down. "So y'all can stay."

Girls ain't usually allowed in this class. Only boys. Up till this year, the school district wouldn't even let Mr. Jacobs teach this class. They said it was against the law to have single-sex classes. But finally, after two years of fighting with the school board, our school won out. Now we got the only class of its kind in the city. It's called Boy Stuff. It's a tenth-grade elective where boys talk, write, and report on things important to us. Like sex, gangs, money, drugs, living, dying, and yeah, girls.

I pull back my chair, stand on top of my desk, and shout, "Be quiet!"

Jacobs pushes up his glasses and fingers his gray baby locs. "Leave now if you aren't mature enough to handle things."

All thirty of us kids lock our lips and listen up when Jacobs heads for the blackboard.

WHY DO BOYS ALWAYS DOG GIRLS? he writes in blue chalk. Then hot-pink words roll onto the blackboard. HOW COME GIRLS THINK THEY OWN BOYS?

Nobody can hear anything after that, 'cause all thirty of us are talking at once.

Jacobs shouts, "Who wants to go first?"

Anna's hand goes up. "What's the question again?"

"Stu-u-u-pid," Tyrek says.

"Go back to sleep," I yell.

Jacobs points to Ryan Sims.

"Well. It's like this," Ryan says. "Girls, like . . . you know, ummm . . . treat us, like, like, I mean . . ."

Melon-head Marimba covers Ryan's lips with her hands. "Boys dog girls 'cause they dogs," she says, ducking when Ryan takes a swing at her. "Rotten, no-good dogs."

Boys ain't gotta take stuff like that from girls, especially girls that look like Marimba. So I ignore Jacobs banging his fist on the desk and I stand up and say my piece.

"Boys dog girls 'cause y'all let us," I say, making my eyes stay extra long on the girls that I know will do anything a boy wants.

Heavenly Smith's got the biggest brown eyes and the biggest mouth. She don't even let me finish talking. She's on her feet, eyes popped and mouth going a mile a minute. "All y'all boys is dogs," she says, waving her finger around the room. "Y'all big, fat, ugly, stinking, rotten dogs." She fixes her eyes on my boy D'Little.

Jacobs reminds everybody that his class ain't

about negativity. "It's about growth." He turns to me and tells me to finish making my comments. I tell the class that girls just get stuck on stupid when they fall for boys. "They believe what you tell 'em—anything."

D'Little jumps in after me. "Far as I'm concerned, girls want boys to treat 'em bad. Otherwise, why they keep letting the same thing happen to 'em over and over again, even when they with a different dude?"

Girls are just too emotional. That's what I think. So they going off on us boys again— Heavenly especially. She's still mad that D'Little dumped her last semester, so every chance she gets, she's on his case. Jacobs takes her hand and leads her over to his desk. "Ms. Smith. Your next step is out that door." He points.

Jacobs's shiny black penny loafers move through the room, stepping over backpacks and big feet. "Jonathan," Jacobs says, sitting down next to him. "Why don't girls know what boys really want? How they really feel?"

Jonathan is smart. Got hisself a 4.2 average. Ain't got no girl, though. "I don't know," he says, not looking Jacobs in the eyes.

Jacobs stays put. He asks him again.

Jonathan taps his fingers on his desk like he's typing out what he's gonna say. "Girls think they know what they want until they get it. Then when it ain't right, instead of ditching it like an old skirt that don't fit no more, they let out the seam, dye it, or try to change it into something it's not." His fingers stop moving. His voice drops. "Then they complain about it not fitting and stuff."

Nobody says nothing for a minute. I mean, we all surprised, especially us boys, 'cause Jonathan got it right.

"Who agrees with Jonathan on this one?" Jacobs asks. Almost everybody's hand goes up. "Then how come boys like Jonathan can't get no play?"

It takes five whole minutes for Jacobs to settle us back down after that one.

Marimba answers the question first. "He's too nice."

"Boring," another girl shouts.

Jacobs goes and sits by Marimba. "Give me more," he says.

Her thumb goes in her mouth, then comes out wet and wrinkled. "You can feel the scared coming off boys like him," she says.

Heavenly butts in. "Like a force field or some-thing."

That's it. Everybody is loud and laughing now. Making it so Jacobs gotta flick the lights off and on and tell three girls to leave the room. By the time class is over, Jacobs reminds us again that tomorrow we won't be just talking about relationships. "We're gonna be testing 'em out, like new cars fresh off the showroom floor."

D'Little asks if that means he gets to kiss Michelle's pretty brown lips. "Or rub Denise's . . ."

Jacobs throws an eraser at him. "Mr. D'Little," he says, "you can put your arms to good use right now—wipe off all three boards. As for your lips," Jacobs says, tapping the floor with his new shoes, "well, the floor could use a little cleaning too."

Jacobs teaches the kind of class you think about four periods before you gotta go to it. So in biology class the next day, me and D'Little already trying to figure out what Jacobs gonna have us doing when we get to his class two periods from now. Heavenly sits near us, and even though we aren't talking to her, she got plenty to say. D'Little asks her very nicely to mind her own business. But he the one that gets kicked outta class when she goes off on him. Saying he said something inappropriate to her. Our teacher, Mr. Pillo, always takes the girls' side. He don't know that Heavenly used to go with D'Little. That she's mad at him all the time now, 'cause she paid $400 for a gown to the ninth-grade ball and he never did show up to take her.

Jacobs is a short, skinny man with an itty-bitty head. But he walks around the room like he is seven feet tall. Arms folded, mouth wide open, clapping his hands whether we say something he likes or doesn't like.

"Mr. D'Little," Jacobs says when D'Little walks into his room late. "Hall pass, please."

D'Little pulls the balled-up pass out his back pocket. "Heavenly's gonna get hurt, Jacobs. I'm telling you."

Jacobs takes him aside and settles him down. Then he tosses the hall pass into the trash and walks over to the window and pulls it wide open. "We are going to try something that's never been done in this school before." He goes to the next window and lifts. "And please, people," he says, picking up a paper blown onto the floor, "don't give me any lip."

In the course description for this class, it says that boys will learn to interact better with girls by engaging in something called "an arrangement." I remember that part because my mother had problems with it at first. Then Jacobs explained things. "Young men today think dating is about finding a girl, mounting a girl, and ditching a girl," he told her. "I want them to see there's more to it than that."

I almost didn't take this class because of that part. I mean, what right does a teacher have to be messing round with your personal business anyhow? But my mother liked what Jacobs said about a man being more than the sum of his parts. I didn't get it, myself. But my mother did, and she signed me up before I had my mind made up good.

Jacobs and the teacher next door worked it so that girls can take part in the class for the next four weeks. The girls are getting paired up with the boys. I know the girl I want. But Jacobs got other ideas. He's sitting on his desk, reading names off a list. He points, and a girl goes and sits by a boy. He points again, and a boy drags his feet, holds his head down, and walks over to a girl with gold highlights in her hair. Dog barks and cat hisses fly through the air when somebody gets hooked up with an ugly girl or some dude that stinks or can't match his clothes.

"Aw, no, man. Please?" D'Little says, when Jacobs takes Marimba by the arm and stands her between him and me.

Jacobs tells us to accept the partner he gives us, or take an F for the course.

I speak up then 'cause I don't want no ugly girl for my partner neither. "This ain't India or Africa, Mr. Jacobs. This here's America. We got the right to pick the person we wanna hook up with."

Jacobs is the golf coach. His thick brown fingers feel like pliers when he takes hold of my neck. "Mr. Wilson, if you don't close your mouth . . ."

Marimba eyes me and D'Little. "You don't know nothing about Africa. 'Cause if you did, you'd know your family would have to pay money, a dowry, for you to marry me." She puts her hand out. "Money. Cash. Lots of it too."

I look at Marimba and bust out laughing—the whole class does. First off, because she's wrong. It's the woman's family that pays a dowry to the man's. Secondly, 'cause nobody would pay money for her. I mean, ain't nothing pretty 'bout Marimba except her name. She's a short, stubby thing that plays b-ball, baseball, and tennis. She looks like a dude in her baggy pants, giant shirts, and zigzag braids, so that's what we call her most times—"dude."

D'Little looks at Marimba and tells Jacobs there's no way he's gonna partner with somebody that looks like her. Marimba slams her fist into his right shoulder. His knees buckle.

I shake my head. "Jacobs hooked you up with a dude, man."

Jacobs asks the girl next to me to move over, and he stands Marimba in her place. "This here's your fiancée," he tells me.

Everybody laughs, except me.

I tell Jacobs that I ain't *never* gonna hook up with Marimba, even if it's just for pretend.

He gets loud. "Don't like it? Leave."

For the next twenty minutes, we all take what we get. No complaints. Then Jacobs explains what he's really up to. "Boys and girls in this country can date anyone they like. So today Jack's dating Jill, but tomorrow he's kissing Jill's best friend and trying to get next to her cousin."

D'Little slaps his chest. "He's talking 'bout me, y'all."

Jacobs keeps talking. "We're going to spend the

next few weeks seeing just what you all know about making relationships work *well*."

He assigns each couple a recorder, someone who will follow them around and give the couple feedback about how well they communicate, respect one another, and manage finances—three key ingredients to a successful relationship, so Jacobs says.

If the couple doesn't do something the way the recorder thinks they should, the couple loses points. Kenya Adams is our recorder. That's messed up too, 'cause I been liking Kenya since forever and here she is gonna decide if I'll make a good boyfriend or not.

"Yo, Jacobs," I say, walking up to him. "Hook me up with Kenya?"

Jacobs is sitting at his desk, writing. The fat gold bracelet he always wears drags across the paper right behind his little brown fingers. "No."

I look over at Kenya and wonder why Jacobs didn't see that he shoulda hooked me up with that.

Jacobs meets with the recorders while he makes us take our fiancées into the halls to get to know them better. I turn my back to Marimba when we get out there. She hits me in the head with her fist. "You . . . you ain't all that good-looking neither, you know."

I try not to let on it hurts. "Whatever," I say. "So what we supposed to do?"

She hunches her shoulders, then slides spearmint gum into her mouth. Her and me, we stand around looking at our feet. Then Kenya comes our way, smiling.

Kenya could be a model. She's, like, five-foot ten, got enough boobs for two and a half girls, perfect teeth, big eyes, and a butt so round your hands just naturally wanna touch it.

"Hi," she says. "I'm your recorder."

"And?" Marimba says.

"And, well, I'm gonna follow you around. But I gotta tell you the rules first." Kenya leans against the wall and sighs. "You and Marimba have to 'work toward a common goal,'" she says, reading off the paper. "'Like completing a paper on this class, buying a house together through the ads in the newspaper, or adopting your recorder.'"

"What?" we both say.

Kenya smiles. "That's what Jacobs says. You two can adopt me for your project. You have to research how to adopt somebody on the Internet. Then adopt me, if that's what I want."

"That's what I want," I say, moving closer to her.

Marimba's pissed, and we ain't been together ten whole minutes. "Why we wanna adopt *you?*"

Kenya reads from the paper. "'Before the couple can say yes or no to any of these options, they must meet and discuss them alone. Recorders may not advise them.'"

Marimba pulls me by the arm and drags me over to the stank-smelling water fountain nobody drinks from. "Listen, we ain't adopting her."

"You just jealous."

Marimba sets me straight, telling me that she's part of this couple and she ain't adopting no big-behind girl. I look back at Kenya with her shiny brown hair and big butt. "Whatever," I say, opening the door and heading back into class.

Jacobs makes us stand by our girls, then dumps, like, a hundred rings on the table. Real ones. He got 'em on the cheap from Goodwill, he says. The diamonds are dulled and the gold is faded on most of 'em, but the girls still act like they're new from the store.

"Remember, boys, your recorder is taking notes. If you just shove that thing on your girl's finger—well, that's ten points. If you kneel down and propose, that's fifty points."

I smack my forehead. "Why you doing this, man?"

Jacobs walks to the back of the room. "Two hundred points for the couple that does the best proposal. All right now. Your recorders have numbers on their papers. It tells which couple goes first, second, third, etc."

Marimba and I are couple number ten, so we have a long time to figure out what to do. The girl's bossy, so she keeps telling me how I should propose to her. I shut her down, though. Told her I was the man. That I was gonna do it the way I wanted. So I did.

"Marimba and Brandon," Jacobs says. "Your turn."

I walk up to the front of the room, trying to be cool. Marimba sits down in a chair and crosses her legs. She's nervous. Her foot keeps shaking.

I clear my throat, turn my back to the class, and think about Kenya. I start off wrong, though. "I'm only doing this 'cause I have to," I tell Marimba.

"Oh, no he didn't," one of Marimba's friends says.

I keep talking. Looking right at Kenya. "I really want this other girl."

Everybody laughs. Not Marimba. She is sitting like a statue, staring at her feet.

I keep going. "I need a girl," I say, looking over at Kenya. "Not a dude."

Marimba bends down and ties her dirty, loose sneaker strings. "Mr. Jacobs, this boy ain't gonna be my fiancé."

Jacobs tells her we have to get engaged. "Right now."

I look at Kenya again, then I hand the ring to Marimba. "Here."

"You supposed to put it on my finger. And propose, too."

I slide it on her left middle finger. "Will you . . ." I say, turning to Jacobs.

"Go ahead," she says.

"Marry me," I say under my breath.

Marimba does what all the girls do when they get the rings on, she holds it up in the air, smiles, and wiggles her fingers.

I walk away. Jacobs shakes his head. Kenya writes the number ten on our paper. That's the lowest score you can get. "Pathetic," she says.

"If it was you," I say, cornering her, "I'd get down on my knees and beg."

* * *

Marimba and me are the worst couple in the world—even Kenya says that. We fight and argue all the time. Jacobs says there are real couples out there who do just that. "And they get married any-how." Our goal, he says, is to try to be more sup-portive of one another's differences. But how am I supposed to do that? I don't like the girl—period. I like tall, sweet-smelling girls who wear clothes as tight as skin. So every day I tell Marimba the same thing—dress up a little. "Put some nail polish on and do your hair every once in a while." Every day her answer is the same: "Screw you!"

Kenya told us the other day that we're gonna fail this part of the class, and she will too, unless Marimba and me do better. "Brandon, this class ain't about how Marimba looks or dresses. It's about relationships, and relationships ain't got nothing to do with clothes."

I can't make them girls understand. A boy's got his reputation. If a boy's got a woman, he wants her to look like something.

We're sitting on the floor outside Jacobs's class before school starts. Kenya called the meeting. Said we needed to get on the ball, or she was gonna ask to be assigned to another couple.

"You two are supposed to buy a house. Here's the paper. Let's start now."

Marimba and me look through the ads together. The whole time, I'm checking out her long Big Bird–looking tube socks.

"Brandon, what kind of house do you want?"

"A house. Any house."

Marimba wants a house with an eat-in kitchen. "I can burn some pots and pans."

I look at her. "You cook?"

She smiles. "Yeah. I help my mom cater." She scratches her head, then checks out the stuff left under her nails. "Gonna have my own catering business one day."

Kenya steps in. "So y'all's house is gonna need a really big stove."

"And a patio for grilling," Marimba says.

The girls in my family cook. The men drink brewskies and watch the games. "We gonna need a family room with a wide-screen TV," I say. "And a pool."

Funny I said that. It turns out that Marimba's on a city swim team. Every morning at 5:30 she's at the pool doing laps.

Marimba and me stay a little longer and pick out our house. It is a three-story colonial, whatever that means, on the north side of town. It's got five bedrooms and two baths, 'cause Marimba wants to have five babies. Before we are done, D'Little comes up to me. "Yo, Brandon. Your girl. She's just . . . ill."

Marimba looks at me like I'm supposed to take up for her. I do. I don't know why, but I do. I tell D'Little to shut his face. "You ain't so hot looking neither. Anyhow," I say, surprising my own self, "long as me and Marimba gotta be together, ain't nobody gonna dog her."

Later Kenya walks up to me and hands me some bonus bucks. She says Jacobs made it so couples can earn extra points and dollars for doing the unexpected. You can lose points and dollars that way, too. For the next two weeks I'm trying to think of stuff to do to get some extra dough. It don't work. Kenya says I'm not being sincere. But all my trying paid off in another way: Kenya is talking to me more often. We are in three other classes together. Before they start, me and her talk about Jacobs's class. We talk about other stuff too—personal stuff. One day it got so good she wrote her phone number on my arm. She said for me not to tell nobody 'cause recorders can't have one-on-one relationships with any one person that makes up a couple. "'Otherwise,'" she quotes, "'the group loses points.'"

The only person I told about me and Kenya was D'Little. He told six other boys in our room, "accidentally," he says. I'm hoping Jacobs don't find out. But mostly, I'm hoping Kenya don't. Otherwise she won't have nothing to do with me . . . again!

Jacobs is getting on my nerves. I'm ready for this engagement mess to end. I've been at it four weeks, and now he's wanting us to make regular progress reports. Halfway through the presentations, he starts writing on the blackboard.

DOES A COMMITTED RELATIONSHIP MEAN THE SAME THING TO GIRLS AND BOYS/MEN AND WOMEN?

Hands go up and mouths start moving.

"Tyrek, speak," Jacobs says. "Then let's hear from your woman," he says, meaning his fiancée.

Tyrek moves his chair away from Olivia. "She ain't my woman, man." Then he starts talking 'bout how guys are like lions—they supposed to roam free and have lots of females at their disposal.

Olivia says that girls are more committed because they were born to be mothers, so they are wired to find lifelong mates, not just the boy with the cutest face or the nicest butt.

I raise my hand and say that makes a lot of sense. Then I ask Jacobs how marriages and engagements are supposed to work if men and women want two different things.

"Yeah, man, I mean, I don't wanna hook up with nobody—for long," D'Little says, holding out his arms like wings. "I gotta spread myself around. Pollinate the place, you know."

Marimba's hand goes up. "How come in nature it's the male animal—like peacocks—that's gotta be extra pretty to get the woman. But with people, it's the girl that's got to do all the work to get a boy?"

I wanna tell her not to worry. Ain't nothing she can ever do to make herself look good.

Jacobs checks out the time, then says class is almost done, so he'll make this quick. "You, you, and you," he says pointing to me, D'Little, and Tyrek, "would get absolutely no play in the animal kingdom."

The class goes off.

"You're not cute enough," he says, busting on us. "Or tall or muscular enough."

Kenya points out that things in nature are different because all male and female animals want to do is procreate—"Make babies so their species don't die out."

I wouldn't mind her having my baby, I think. Once the bell rings, I go up to her and ask if she wants to go to the movies. Marimba is nearby, so Kenya ignores me. Later on, she walks up to me and says she'll go. "But Marimba's gotta go, too. Jacobs's rules. Recorders can't be alone with one member of the couple."

I wanna tell her to forget it at first. But she says she'll sit next to me. "And, well, Marimba ain't gotta know everything."

All day long I'm thinking 'bout that girl. Feeling sorry for Marimba, kinda, too. I mean, I'm supposed to be her fiancé. And I don't even give her no play, not even for pretend. That's messed up. But Jacobs shouldn't have hooked me up with her. She ain't my type.

We all agree to meet at the movies at Ninth and Oak at nine o'clock. I'm there waiting when Kenya calls my cell and says she got stuck taking care of her brothers, so she can't come. Now I'm stuck with Marimba.

For a while I try to figure out how to get out of this movie deal. But Marimba's dad drops her off and, well, I don't wanna tell no man the size of the Statue of Liberty that I'm ditching his daughter. But the whole while we're watching the movie, I'm checking my cell, hoping Kenya calls. I'm excusing myself and going to the bathroom, calling Kenya and talking to her five, ten, fifteen minutes at a time. Kenya keeps saying that I'm doing Marimba wrong, but she don't hang up on me.

Marimba is boiling mad. After I leave her for the ninth time, she calls her dad and tells him to come get her. I don't stick around. I'm gone before she is. Kenya tells me I'm gonna lose points for the way I treated her. "Fiancées can't be mistreated. Jacobs's rules."

"I don't care," I say, "as long as I don't lose no points with you."

"One more week," Jacobs says. "And this is the final test."

D'Little and me standing by each other. He says

this has been the worst three weeks of his life. "And I ain't never getting married neither."

I slap him five. Jacobs lets us know that things are gonna get worse, not better. I look over at Marimba. She ain't spoke to me since the movie thing last weekend. I don't care really, but Kenya deducts fifteen points for every day we two don't communicate. Marimba and me gonna fail this project if she keeps this up.

"You can double your total points this week," Jacobs says. "If you decide not to do what I'm asking, you'll lose four hundred points—which is half of all the points you can earn." Jacobs heads my way. "That happens, and there's no way you can earn higher than a C for the course."

Everybody tells him that's not fair.

"I'm not trying to be fair, here," he says, wiping chalk off his hands. "I'm trying to teach you about relationships—none of which is fair, *boys and girls.*"

I like what Jacobs says we have to do. Marimba looks like she wants to cry.

"Gonna have to change them clothes, huh?" I say. "Buy you a dress or skirt or something," I say, laughing.

Kenya explains the rules. Me and Marimba

have to pick something we don't like about one another. Each person has to do what the other wants for one whole week. I knew right off that I was gonna tell Marimba to get rid of them clothes and get her hair did. But me, I dress like a king. I smell like heaven and I got the best cut in this school, so there's nothing she can ask me to change. Even Marimba can't think of nothing for me to do differently, till Kenya whispers in her ear.

"Be nice to me," Marimba says.

"I am nice to you."

She shakes her head.

"She means, open doors for her."

I shake my head no.

"Pull out chairs for her when y'all in class together."

"What?"

Marimba's liking what she's hearing. "And . . . and tell me I'm cute in front of your boys."

I shake my head no. "That ain't the kind of stuff Jacobs was talking about."

Kenya puts up her hand and Jacobs comes over. He laughs after she explains our conversation. "Yep. You have to do it, if Marimba wants you to."

"She trying to make a fool outta me."

"You already a fool," Kenya says, walking off with Marimba.

I walked right by Marimba. Didn't even recognize the girl. She had to take hold of my arm and ask me how come I didn't speak to her. My mouth fell open. "That your hair?" I asked. "Your clothes?"

This is the first time I ever saw Marimba in shoes—girl shoes—with high heels and pretty colors. She got nice legs, too. "Man," I say. "You look awright."

Kenya clears her throat. "How she look?"

I know what she's doing. "You look pretty," I say, low enough for my boys not to hear.

All during class I stare at Marimba. She's pulling at her short pink skirt—grabbing hold of her collar top and snapping her bra straps.

"All this time," D'Little says, "I thought the girl was a dude. And here she got more up top than any girl in this class."

I just stare at her.

"That her real hair, you think?" D'Little asks.

I ain't sure. She always wore braids or her hair under a cap. And here it is, straight and black and down past her shoulders. "She still walk like a dude," I say when she goes to sharpen a pencil.

D'Little follows her with his eyes. So do most of the other boys. "I like the legs," he says. "The butt ain't bad neither."

Kenya whispers in my ear. I don't want to do it, but before Marimba sits down I go over to her and pull her chair out. Everybody laughs, even Jacobs. Marimba knocks her book on the floor, on purpose, I think. I pick it up. I woulda left it down there, but I need the points, and Kenya's watching.

"In three days, you will have to turn in a written assignment," Jacobs says. "I hope you've been keeping careful records. Class dismissed."

When Marimba gets to the door, I open it without anybody telling me to. D'Little says I'm pathetic. Heavenly asks how come I didn't hold it open for her. "'Cause I ain't no butler," I say.

Everybody's teasing me. Calling me "Mr. Manners." Asking how come I'm waiting on Marimba hand and foot. I tell 'em it ain't something I wanna do. I gotta do it for class. Only it ain't as bad as I thought, opening doors for girls, pulling their chairs out. Besides, the more I do it, the more girls be coming up to me and talking to me. Girls that never paid me no attention are giving me a little play now. This girl Elizabeth made me stop and talk to her. She was all up in my face. Kenya saw it and deducted fifty points. I'm starting to wonder about that girl.

Jacobs walks through the aisles collecting our final papers. "Recorders come to the front, please."

Ten students go up front. It's funny, I never realized that half the recorders were boys and half were girls. And they are the cutest, or best dressed, or most popular kids in school, too. When Jacobs joins them up front, he explains why those kids got picked in the first place.

"In relationships, there are lots of distractions. The pretty girl," he says, standing next to Kenya. "The jock," he says, pretending to throw a left hook to Kevin, who heads the football team. "People with a big chest, pretty eyes, or nice hair."

Jacobs says the recorders were placed in our groups to distract us from our mission. He asks the recorders to raise their hands if they were able to make one or both people pay more attention to them than their fiancés. Eight hands go up.

"Kenya," Jacobs says. "Explain."

Kenya tells all my business. How I tried to hit

on her. How I paid her more attention than Marimba. "And when I didn't show up for the movies like you told me, Jacobs, he didn't even talk to Marimba."

Marimba raises her hand. She called Kenya that night, she says, 'cause she was hurt I didn't say one word to her during the movies. "I know he doesn't like me, but he coulda at least treated me decent."

I'm pissed. This whole thing was a setup from the start. "Wasn't no way I could be a good fiancé, Jacobs. Everything you did made it so I'd mess up."

Jacobs settles me down. Then D'Little's recorder gives a report. Another pretty girl saying almost the same thing Kenya said about me. "Listen, Jacobs," D'Little says. "A boy's gonna try and talk to a looker. That's just how it is."

The girls get mad at that, but the boys clap— 'cause they know it's true.

Jacobs hits the board again. ALL BOYS ARE DOGS THEN, RIGHT?

I'm expecting Kenya, Marimba, and the rest of the girls to say, Yep! But Kenya's singing a different tune. Telling Jacobs under the right circumstances anyone could cheat—be a dog.

Jonathan's fiancée raises her hand. She says she

didn't have one bit of trouble out of him. "He's a gentleman."

"A nerd," I say.

Kenya speaks up again. "Maybe people cheat or look around when they know better's out there for them."

Marimba ain't buying that. She says couples have to learn to work out their problems. Not sniff after someone else when things get rough.

I wanna tell the whole class that this was a project, an experiment, not no real relationship. But Marimba's got a point. So does Kenya. When you ain't happy, it's easy to go sniffing. But do that make it right?

Jacobs picks on the girls, too. A lot of 'em tried to hit on *their* recorders. It was different for them, though. They called the boys day and night. Spread rumors about 'em when they didn't give 'em no play.

"Brandon," Jacobs says, pointing my way. "Learn anything, buddy?"

"No," I say at first. But once everyone's done laughing, I tell him what he wants to hear. "I learned that relationships are hard work."

He's smiling. I'm not. I'm thinking about Kenya.

How she played me—used me, even. But then it hits me; I used Marimba. When class is over and everybody is gone, I ask Jacobs why he made us do all of this in the first place. "Everybody used everybody else in our group."

"Did you like being used?"

"Naw, man."

"Remember that," he says, wiping chalk off the board, "when you hook up with a girl next time."

I slap him five and head for the door. Before I'm halfway up the hall, Elizabeth is hunting me down to give me her phone number. I take it. But I don't know if I'll call her. Not just yet, anyhow.

I Know a Stupid Boy When I See One

WILLIE GREENTEA'S GONNA hurt me bad one day. I told that to my daddy, Mable Lee, and that rich lawyer woman from way 'cross town. Ain't nobody do nothing to stop him, though. But I ain't surprised. They never cared about me nohow. It was my baby they all wanted. He's fine now. But me, I'm here suffocating. Watching my life pass right in front of me just like in the movies. Dying ain't so bad, I guess, but it is kind of lonely. And your mind don't stay put neither. All I keep thinking 'bout is God, and what He thinks about me—a sixteen-year-old single mother who tried to sell her baby for hardly nothing.

Truth is, girls 'round my way get pregnant all the time. Heck, I'm old compared to most. But in my

daddy's house, a pregnant girl is like a roach crawling 'cross the kitchen table—something you best
get rid of 'fore the neighbors spot it. So soon as
Daddy found out about me, he tossed me out. I ain't
have no place to sleep for two weeks. Then Momma
talked him into letting me back in the house. A
month later, when my belly was still flat as notebook paper, my father sat me down and said something good was gonna come outta this here mess I
stirred up. That's when he stuck a little card in my
hand. Said a white woman was handing 'em out at
the check-cashing store on Eighth Avenue.

"Twelve thousand dollars for brand-new
babies," he said.

Momma and me tried to interrupt, but Daddy
kept talking. "This lawyer uses the Internet, and
gets people from all over the world to bid on
babies." He stared in his hands like the money was
already there. "Seems fair enough," he said. "A couple gets a baby, and we get paid."

I didn't want to give up my baby. But when I
told my boyfriend, Oscar, about Daddy's plan, he
was all for it. "Too many babies 'round our way
now," he wrote me from jail. "Ain't never enough
dough."

146

Anyhow, that's how I got to Mable Lee's, where gals like me end up selling their babies like lettuce from the back of a pickup truck.

The first day that lawyer woman brought me to Mable Lee's place, Willie Greentea was standing on the front porch picking his nose. I know a stupid boy when I see one, and I could tell right off that Willie didn't have much upstairs. You could see it in his eyes. They was as empty as the hallway at school soon after the last bell rings. But I was nice to him right off. I introduced myself. Stood so close he could smell the ginger spice perfume I had rubbed all over me and see the purple specks in my pretty green eyes. Shoot, even boys with all their marbles can't resist looking at my eyes for longer than they should. Willie wasn't no different. He stared at me so long that first day, it scared me. But I moved closer to him anyhow. Asked if he liked how I smelled.

He nodded his jug head. "Yeah."

"How 'bout my eyes. You like them too?" I said, knowing full well that boys is crazy 'bout light-skinned gals with eyes like mine.

He almost poked me in the left one. "They yours?"

I smacked his dirty hand. "How else I'm gonna get 'em? Buy 'em at the corner store like candy?"

Dumb boys ask a whole lot of stupid questions. Ten minutes later, Willie was still asking 'bout my eyes. Cuss words started flying out my mouth 'fore I thought about it good. Next thing I knew, Mable Lee was dragging me in the house by the arm. Telling me that kinda language ain't got no place 'round here. I was glad she took me away from Willie Greentea that day. Wish she'd-a snatched me off that front porch long before I ever met him.

I could tell right off that Mable Lee wasn't like the other women 'round here that have to do day's work to make ends meet. First off, she got porch furniture, not no broke-down couch sitting out front her place like most folks. And she got new windows and pretty, white-laced curtains hanging up everywhere.

I put my suitcase down and rubbed my hand over the cool, hard plastic covering the green sofa.

"I'm-a do like you when I grow up," I said, looking 'round the room.

"How's that?" she said, picking up the used blue suitcase that lawyer woman gave me and heading up the stairs.

"I'm gonna make money off kids too, so I ain't gotta work and my bills get paid on time."

Mable Lee stopped on the eighteenth step. She turned her big hips around and laid me out. Didn't use not one cuss word, neither. But I tell you this, I ain't never been told off like *that* before. When she started up the steps again, she let me know that she took in girls like me 'cause the Lord closed up her private parts, not 'cause she wanted money to pay off her house. Then she walked up the rest of the stairs in silence, went into the bedroom, and sat on the bed to catch her breath. "Would do it for free, if I had to."

"But you don't," I said, sitting down next to her. Counting all the knobs on the dressers in the room.

Mable Lee ain't talk to me for a while after that. She just showed me around the upstairs. Then told me I was responsible for washing my own clothes and doing the dishes every night after supper. When she mentioned something 'bout a curfew, I laughed.

"What a pregnant gal need a curfew for? Ain't nothing she can do that she ain't already done," I said, trying to keep my lips still while I counted the hairs on her chin.

Mable Lee shook her head, then opened the closet and handed me a present—a smooth, white box with pink ribbon tied around it. "Welcome," she said, sitting it on my lap.

I ain't even say thanks. I pulled off the ribbon. Dumped the clothes on the bed. Counted every piece. "I don't need no pregnant clothes," I said, getting mad. "I got too many now." I threw the box way 'cross the room. "I need other stuff, too, you know."

Mable Lee's voice got as small and tight as the gold ring on her baby finger. "It's just a little something to say welcome."

I walked over to the window and stared at Willie Greentea sitting on his back porch rocking. I thought, He'll buy me stuff. Pretty, tight things.

Mable Lee came over and shook me good. "He a good boy. You stay away from him."

I stared at Willie Greentea with his long skinny head and droopy eyes. I like boys like him, I wanted to tell Mable Lee. Slow, stupid boys. They give you anything you want, and you ain't hardly gotta do nothing to get it, neither. I smiled. "I can't help it if boys like me."

She shook her head. Pulled up the corner of her

wig and scratched. "Slick slides on its own grease," she said, taking her own good time walking over to the door. "Watch you don't *bust your head* on your way down."

Mable Lee is like that. Always talking in riddles. Saying stuff that don't make much sense. That's why I didn't tell her for the longest time that Willie Greentea was after me. Anyhow, if I woulda told her, I woulda had to tell her he was buying me stuff too. Stealing it when he ain't have no money. And wasn't no way I was gonna tell Mable Lee nothing like that. She go to church every now and then—and stealing is something she just can't abide.

It wasn't no time 'fore I had Willie Greentea wrapped 'round my finger like a good-luck string. "I sure could use me something to drink," I said one day.

He looked at me. Squeezed his big hands down in his pants pockets and pulled out some bills. I left the store with two cream sodas, three bags of chips, and ten one-dollar bills. I barely had to ask Willie for that money. I kissed him on the cheek after I got it. Boys like Willie don't get kissed by nobody 'cept their mommas, so they'll do just 'bout anything if you give 'em a peck every now and then. Might even hurt somebody, if you ask.

Mable Lee asked more than once where I got some new ring or the few extra dollars she saw in the bottom of my drawer. I always lied. Told her Oscar sent me things. Never did say he was in jail. Never said he was white, neither. It wasn't none of her business. So I kept on taking from that other boy. Kept asking him for more and more. Momma says that poor women don't have nothing but a bunch of babies and blistered fingers by the time you lay 'em in the grave. "So if you can get some extras, get 'em, 'cause God knows I ain't never had nothing more than hard times and empty hands," she told me.

My momma's white. So that means this here baby's gonna be extra light. "Close to white," the lawyer woman said. "Couples pay more for babies like that. Two thousand more than the rest."

Daddy liked that. "Finally, a little good luck."

I wondered 'bout the other babies. The ones that was one hundred percent black. Do they get good homes, too, or do they get gypped twice—worth less money right from the start, then put in second-rate homes to boot?

I was thinking on this the day Willie's daddy came to Mable Lee's place hunting me down like a crook who stole his last dollar. Saying for me to stay away from Willie. I told him that it wasn't me who couldn't stay away from Willie, but Willie who couldn't get enough of me.

His father kept talking. Telling me that Willie wasn't stupid, just slow. Willie was seven, he said, when the sense got knocked outta him. "He jumped in the shallow end of the lake, and hit his head on the bottom."

I laughed. I don't know why, but I did.

Mr. Greentea's voice got as rough and hard as the bunions on the bottom of Mable Lee's feet. "'Cause you near white, you think you can treat people like you want; act any way you like, huh?"

I gave him the finger.

His fingers curled like fatback in hot grease, then loosened and took hold of my neck.

For a minute I stopped breathing—I swear I did. 'Cause I could see that he would really hurt me if he had to. That he would make me disappear like dirty, wet snow after a hard rain if I didn't stay clear of his boy.

* * *

I did just like Willie's daddy said. I stayed away
from Willie. But Willie likes my eyes and the
white in my skin, and he came looking for me. At
first I told him to get. He took off like a cat sprayed
with a hose. The next two times he left right away,
but snuck back later and left me a little something by
the door. I liked that. So when he came back the
fourth time I told him we had to keep our friendship
secret. He understood. So we started meeting in the
park, after dark.

Willie Greentea likes it dark. So dark you can't
see nothing, not even the whites in somebody else's
eyes. I didn't know that at first. So when he said
we should walk to the park, I was all for it. I
stopped cold, right before we went in, though. "I
don't know, Willie. How we gonna see anything
with no lights on?"

Willie pulled out a flashlight. Said he liked the
dark better than the daylight. "'Cause you can't
hardly see people staring and pointing at ya."

He took my hand and we went in. Found us a
bench and just sat still for a while. And you know
it wasn't long 'fore my eyes could tell what was
what. So I didn't mind, not at first, us sneaking off

to the park at night. It was fun—him hiding greasy brown paper bags under park benches, behind trees, or right by the creek and making me find 'em. Knowing just what a girl like me wants: a Timex watch that ticks under water, perfume, gold earrings, red lipstick, and money—always money. But then one night, when I went to kiss his cheek for the pretty silk scarf he gave me, he turned his face around. Pushed his lips out as far as he could and said, "Kiss me here."

I took too long, I guess. So Willie just bent over and kissed me. Right on my mouth. Right where Oscar kisses me—where nobody else is supposed to touch me. I went crazy for a minute. Pulling at my lips like I could take 'em off and throw 'em in the creek for cleaning. Smacking Willie upside the head and punching his arms and ignoring my baby kicking me—reminding me, I guess, that I was five months pregnant.

I threw the watch, perfume, and the clip-on earrings in the creek, making sure to keep the money and the lipstick tight in my left hand. Then I started walking—running, really. Next thing I know, Willie's chasing me, grabbing hold of my neck.

Willie's hands are as strong and tight as the twine they twist 'round the fish they gut and wrap in funny papers so you can take 'em home. His fingers closed around my neck and made it so I couldn't hardly breathe.

I whispered. "Don't . . ." and pulled at his long stringy fingers.

"Those my mother's earrings," he said. "She gonna be mad when she know they lost in the water."

I pulled back my arm and slammed my elbow in his belly. He turned me loose and walked into the creek in his shoes and dug in the mud till he found the earrings. "They wasn't gonna be yours for keeps," he said, wiping 'em on his pants. "Just for a little while, till Momma missed 'em too much."

I left Willie in the park holding mud in his hands. He told me to wait up, 'cause he wanted to find the perfume too. But I kept walking. Kept feeling my neck and wondering what made Willie do what he done to me. They was just some plain old earrings—cheap ones, really. Just like all the other things he stole off his mother and said was mine for keeps.

I told Mable Lee what happened. Willie's daddy too. They both said for me to hush my lies.

"Girls like you always trying to take advantage of boys like Willie. Guess every now and then they just get mad, is all."

I thought about what Mable Lee said. Figured maybe it was me that made him do what he did. So I ain't stay away from him, I just didn't ask him for much. Then a month or so later, I went knocking on his door. Him and me ended up in the park after dark. And just like before, his hands ended up on my neck. He was mad all over again 'bout something else this time. I don't even remember what. I ran straight to his daddy. I forgot I still had on Willie's momma's new pearl earrings. They got snatched off my ears, that's for sure.

"Willie gonna hurt me bad one day," I said while his daddy pulled me down the front steps. "Y'all just watch and see."

His father dragged me to Mable Lee's place and told her he was gonna call the state on her if she didn't keep no-good trash like me from hangin' 'round his son. "They use him. Then lie on him when it suits 'em."

I wrapped my arms 'round Mable Lee. "Willie Greentea gonna hurt me bad, Mable Lee. I know he is."

She told Willie's father not to worry 'bout me
no more. After he left, she said she was gonna call
my father. Let him know I was trying to mess
things up for everybody. My daddy ain't believe me
neither. He said I was just trying to be slick, trying
to stir the pot and keep trouble brewing.

I kept to myself after that. I stayed in the house
for the next three weeks. Mable Lee said I was
nesting. "Making ready for the baby." I didn't tell
her no different. I read year-old magazines. Paid
close attention when she taught me to knit. And
gave my baby a name I knew he wasn't never gonna
use: Isaiah. Then one day Oscar sent me a letter. He
was getting outta jail soon and said he was mad
about the baby and what my daddy was doing.
Only he wasn't mad about the adoption. Just about
my father getting more money out the deal than us.
I wrote him back that same day.

Dear Oscar,
     Don't worry. We'll get our due. Check your mail
next week. I'm sending you more money.

The next day I went over Willie's place.
Mostly I went there for Oscar. But I went for me

too. My belly was getting bigger. My feet had swelled up two sizes and I was ready for somebody to tell me I was pretty again. Besides, Willie ain't mean no harm, I told myself.

Willie's parents' car was gone two hours by then. So I knocked on the front door and let myself in. Willie was sitting in the living room in the dark. I cut on the light. Rubbed my big belly and sat down beside him.

"Where do babies go?" he asked.

I fanned myself. "Where do babies come from, you mean?"

He shook his head no. "Where they go?" He walked over to me, bent down, and put his sweaty head on my belly. "Where they go once they come outta ya?" His face got sad like tears were gonna come next. "All Mable Lee's babies go away for good. The girls do too."

I stared down at Isaiah. Then explained to Willie why girls like me come here in the first place.

"I got babies too," he said, heading upstairs. He had a shoe box in his hand when he got back.

I screamed before he had the top off good.

Six baby birds—all dead. Two yellow chicks, hard and stiff as raw spaghetti. Sixteen butterflies, baby bees, two tadpoles, and a baby mouse—legs stuck in the air like toothpicks with feet.

He rubbed one of the dead chicks. "I like babies."

"Not me," I lied.

He sat a baby bird in his hand. "They was already broken when I got 'em."

I stood up, held on to my belly like he could stuff Isaiah in that box too. "I gotta go."

His hand pressed my stomach so I couldn't go nowhere. "Is it broke already?"

I just looked at him.

"I wasn't broke at first," he said, taking his other hand and fingering his face and head. "Then I jumped in the pond, and the ground hit me in the head." His hands went back to my belly. "Don't let the ground hit him, okay?"

"He's mine now," I told Willie. "But soon he'll be somebody else's." Then I explained how I was being paid for the baby.

Willie's slow all right. 'Cause even after twenty minutes of trying to make him understand, he still didn't get it. After I was done, he closed up his box and took his sweet time walking up the stairs. A few minutes later, he came back down with his mother's pink knit purse. He handed me some dollar bills and a jar full of change.

"This is for the baby."

I was glad for the money, so I took every cent. Before I was out the door though, Willie asked, "It's mine now, right?"

I stared at him, then at my belly.

"But don't break it," he said, "'cause I don't want no more broken babies."

My hand turned the knob. His hand took hold of mine.

"I bought it . . . the baby . . . so it's really, really mine, right?"

I pulled his fingers off me and headed out the door. "Sure, Willie."

Two days later my water broke and the baby came early. Mable Lee said it was a bad sign. She was right. Things just got worse after that. I changed my mind about passing Isaiah on, and the lawyer woman didn't like it one bit. She phoned Daddy. He phoned me and said if I didn't do like I promised, I couldn't come home. Then I called Oscar. He made a whole lot of sense when he said we could use the money to go live in another town and start over. So I signed the papers.

"Never shoulda named that baby," Momma said. "That just make 'em real."

They kept me in the hospital ten days, 'cause the bleeding wouldn't stop. Willie came by that last day. I was still green under the eyes, and he told me so. Willie said he saw Isaiah through the glass. "I got me a pretty baby," he said, smiling. "Green-eyed and everything."

I wasn't talking much. I was too tired. Willie let me know, though, that Isaiah was his. "Paid for already." He stood over me. "He broken, though. But they say he gonna get fixed."

I told him Isaiah was gonna be good as new soon. "But he's going away. We ain't gonna see him no more."

You gotta tell Willie Greentea some things twice. So I repeated myself. He went out the door. I heard him at the nurses' station trying to get *his* baby. Telling 'em that he ain't care if it was broken, just so long as they turned it over to him and "not nobody else."

I made Willie come back to my room. I'm sorry now that I did. 'Cause I would still be alive if

I hadn't. It's easy, I guess, to kill people when you ain't got nobody around to make you see things different.

"You lied," Willie said, pushing me into the wall.

I tried not to be scared. "Lied about what, Willie? About what?"

He told me exactly how much money he had paid me for the baby. My fingers covered my mouth. "Oscar got that money. But I can get it back."

Willie don't know Oscar. He didn't care nothing 'bout him neither. He just wanted the baby—his baby. I ain't no fast thinker, so it took me a while to tell him I'd get the baby for him tomorrow. No matter, he ain't believe me. He asked again, real quiet like, for his baby. Then his soft, pretty hands went to my throat.

"You broke it, now you want to keep it too," he said, squashing my voice box with his thumb.

I could hear nurses walking past my room. Feel my fingers scratching at the baby ducks on the wallpaper. "Willie," I heard myself say finally. "Isaiah needs me, Willie."

Willie Greentea smiled. He didn't look broken

then. He looked strong and tall and sweet, even. "I bought him," he said, squeezing harder.

My head was light and fuzzy. And after a while, even though I could feel Willie's fingers on my neck, I couldn't hear what he was saying and I didn't even hurt no more. "One, seven, ten," I said, counting ducks one by one. Then all of a sudden the hospital room disappeared, and me and Mable Lee was sitting in her kitchen sipping dandelion tea. "You think a girl like me could be a angel up in heaven?" I heard myself ask. 'Fore Mable Lee could speak, Daddy pulled up a chair and sat down too. "Don't be silly, gal. God ain't got no use for broken angels."

I was all set to cry after he said that. Then in walks Isaiah. He takes me by the hand and leads me to a room all lit up like Christmas. "It's all right, Momma," he says. "Heaven's got all kinds of angels in it."

Then I hear this twinkling sound, like I'm surrounded by wind chimes. Before I know it, Isaiah's gone, and my throat hurts worse than ever. I look around and Willie's crying, and somebody's doing push-ups on my chest. I close my eyes and head for the Christmas lights, 'cause I wanna find out for myself if Isaiah's right 'bout them angels.

Hunting for Boys

THERE ARE TEN girls my age at the church that I attend, and only one boy. His name is Jeremiah. He carries a Bible everywhere he goes, so we all decided long ago that he was not the one for us.

Our church is small. Only a hundred members on the books. That means maybe forty folks show up each Sunday. So we girls are like sisters. We sleep over at each other's houses, paint one another's nails, and lie for one another when we have to.

We figured God wasn't being fair putting us in a church with just one boy and giving us parents so strict that boys at school are too afraid even to speak to us, let alone ask us to the school's annual Mardi Gras festival. So we got our heads together and decided to change things.

We were in the church basement. Our parents thought we were planning Teen Sunday, which was a few weeks away. But we were really trying to come up with ideas on how to get boys to take us to Mardi Gras. Our parents already said we couldn't go. "Card games, wild dancing, crazy costumes, no way," Pastor said. But we have to go. Everybody goes! And only the losers go without dates.

My friends and I are fourteen years old, in the ninth grade, and this is our first time in public school with regular kids. We went to the church school from K through eighth grade, then the state shut the school down. They said the building didn't meet state code, and our teachers weren't certified, even though we're all three grades ahead of most kids in our new school in math and reading. Anyhow, now we go to school with the neighborhood kids, but we're still not allowed to do like they do or go where they go.

Satina has it worst of all because Pastor's her father. They don't own a TV set or listen to the radio. But Satina still knows how to dance. And she knows all the words to the latest rap songs. Satina made it clear. "I'm going to that festival. And I'm going with a boy!"

China is the one that came up with the best idea for meeting boys. None of us would have figured it, though. She's shy and hardly opens her mouth unless it's to stick gum in it. "The hoop courts. Boys always hang out there."

Satina hugged her. "But we can't go to the ones around here. Everybody knows what my father will do to them if he catches them around us."

I thought about it a while. "Let's just get on a bus and ride till we find one."

Jamaica was scared at first. "Pastor says we can't date until we graduate. And we can't dance. Period."

"'The devil's in that music,'" Satina said, mocking her dad. She cleared her throat three times in a row, same as he does every Sunday morning. "'And the devil ain't gonna have his way with nary a one of you,'" she said, pointing to each girl.

Jamaica told Satina to stop disrespecting Pastor. "We are not supposed to be like everybody else out there, shaking our butts and showing our . . ." She wouldn't say the word. But we all knew what she meant, so we stared at our chests while she talked. "Pastor says it's all there to distract us."

I tried to be smart. "What's there to distract us?"

"You know," Jamaica said, sitting in a chair and squeezing her knees tight like the church sisters taught us.

I knew. Gold jewelry. Tattoos, toe rings, tongue and belly piercings. Tight tops, short skirts, boys with eyes that looked right through you. Dancing . . . sweaty, close dancing in rooms with hardly any light and no adult supervision. I knew, so did Jamaica, China, Satina, N'kia, Karen, Anna Belle, K'ya, Daylea, and Lisa. Pastor tells us all the time. And he's right, I think. Only sometimes, like now, we get tired of missing out.

Satina ignored Jamaica and headed for the stairs. "I'm sick of being cooped up in church all the time. I wanna have some fun," she said so loud I had to cover her mouth with my hand. "Y'all coming?" she asked the rest of us.

One by one we headed for the steps.

"Jamaica. You gotta come," I said.

Jamaica was the only one still sitting down. "God ain't gonna like it. Neither is Pastor."

My eyes went straight up to the cross high up on the wall with Jesus hanging on it. "We don't mean no harm," I said. "But we wanna go to the festival with boys. Just once, anyhow."

China ran over to Jamaica and pulled her hand. "If we do something dumb and you're not there to stop us, God's gonna blame you for it."

Jamaica believed her. She is the oldest, and Pastor and the church sisters always hold her accountable for what the rest of us do. So she came along, too. And that's how all ten girls from the Calvary Church of God's Blessed Example went hunting for boys—and found something a whole lot worse.

"God don't like ugly." That's what my mother always says. So I guess that's why the bus never came to take us to the hoop court. We waited for an hour and a half. By then, Pastor had shown up, wanting to know where we were off to.

"Nowhere," K'ya said, tying her black sneakers at the curb. The rest of us stared at the ground, bit our nails, or scratched places that didn't really itch.

Pastors can read minds, you know. So right then ours gave us a mini sermon on boys. He pointed to a really cute guy on the steps across the street. "I see him looking over here every time you girls step foot in church." He took Satina's hand. "I don't blame him. We got a whole church full of pretty gals."

"Thanks, Pastor," we said, blushing.

"But don't be fooled. That's trouble sitting on that step." He pointed to Jamaica, then to me, K'ya, and finally Satina. "You looking for trouble?"

"No."

"No, sir."

"Pastor, I ain't looking for nothing," K'ya said.

Pastor smiled. "Good. Life has enough trouble without you all chasing it down like a two-for-one shoe sale at the mall."

I wanted to look him in the eyes and say, "Amen," like I do in church sometimes. But I couldn't, 'cause I figured he would see what I was really up to. So I followed him back into the church, like everyone else, and folded paper towels for tomorrow's supper with the congregation from Bethel Hill Church across town.

"Maybe. Maybe we should forget about the festival," Karen said, laying plastic forks and knives on towels. "I mean, if Pastor finds out what we're up to . . ."

Satina looked at her baggy beige skirt. It was below her knees, just like ours. "What's wrong with playing cards or dancing?" she said, pulling her skirt up to the middle of her thighs and turning in circles. "What's wrong with meeting boys and having fun and being normal like other kids?" she asked. She threw some forks on the floor and crushed 'em with her shoe.

"Y'all working down there, or playing?" Pastor asked from the top of the stairs. We shut up and got back to work. But Satina's words stayed in my head. Why can't we be like other girls? Why can't we dance and wear makeup and be with boys—kiss 'em, even? That's what girls our age do. That's all they wanna do, really.

The adult women's choir only has three members, so they make me, China, Satina, Jamaica, and K'ya sing along with them every third Sunday. We sing, but mostly we sit behind Pastor and write notes to each other.

"It's a sign," Jamaica wrote on the back of the church bulletin. "What Pastor said yesterday about boys is a sign from God that He knows what we're up to and He don't like it none."

She was right. All night long I had been thinking the same thing.

"I'm scared God's gonna punish us for going after boys," China wrote.

I tried to tell her God wasn't gonna punish us for just talking to boys. But I didn't tell her that last night in my dream I was kissing one on the lips.

"Jesus sees everything. He knows everything, too," China wrote.

"So He knows you're up to no good," K'ya said in my ear. Then she laughed. I didn't think that was funny.

Satina leaned forward and played with the collar of her starched white shirt. "I don't know if I wanna go now."

Satina's dad prays with her at home every morning. Today, when he was done, he said he knew it wasn't easy being a minister's daughter and he was proud of how she handles herself. Before they left home, he kissed her on the forehead. "You're a good girl," he told her. "No one's ever been able to say different."

K'ya pulled out the bulletin for today and wrote up and down the sides in red ink. "It was your idea, Satina, for us to go meet boys. So don't chicken out now."

Sister Berta grabbed the paper from Satina. "You here to chitchat, or serve the Lord?"

Satina didn't answer.

Sister Berta is seventy-six years old, with brown wrinkled hands that look like beef-stick skins. "Pastor's gonna see how you spend your time up here," she said, eyeing us five. Then she lay the paper in her lap like a handkerchief, and rocked.

Satina looked scared. "Get it back," she said— like K'ya could do something about it. When it was time to sing, Sister Berta stood up and the paper fell to the floor. I grabbed it and handed it to K'ya, who gave it to Satina, who stuck it in her purse right when Sister Berta's mouth opened wide and she started singing off-key:

> Yes, Jesus, yes.
> All that you ask, I will do.
> Show me the way. Make it clear every day.
> And I'll say yes, Lord, yes, yes, ohhh yesss.

"No," I told Karen. We were standing in front of the church, waiting for the bus. "It's coming in a minute, and we can't miss it."

Two weeks after Sister Berta took Satina's note, we stopped being scaredy-cats and headed for the hoop courts again.

When we got on the bus, all we did was talk about boys and the tight, short shorts Satina, K'ya, Lisa, and Daylea had on. They had bought them at the store a few days ago. The rest of us didn't have the nerve.

We sat in the back, so it was easy for them to unzip their long granny skirts, pull them off, and stuff them in their backpacks. But when Satina pulled off her long-sleeved shirt and showed off a pretty orange tube top, Jamaica got loud. She said we weren't allowed to show our legs or go out without proper tops.

Why? I thought, smearing raspberry-red lip gloss on. Our legs are as pretty as any other girl's at school.

Daylea covered her thighs with her skirt. "If it's not in the Bible, God doesn't care if we do it or not, right?"

Jamaica rolled her eyes and turned up the music on her CD player. I asked what she was listening to, and she put her headphones on my ears.

> *Keep me pure, Lord. Keep me pure.*
> *Help me do the things that you adore.*
> *Make me perfect, make me strong.*
> *Keep my eyes on you, where they belong.*

I felt like dirt after hearing that song. So for the rest of the trip I didn't talk much. I watched Jamaica, Karen, and Anna Belle read scripture cards and sing out loud every now and then. And I prayed a little. Asked God not to let me do nothing too wrong while I was out here. But when I wasn't praying, I was thinking about boys. Wondering if they would think I was pretty.

"There's a basketball court!" Anna Belle said, standing up and running to the front of the bus. We ran behind her, almost falling off the bus into the street.

The neighborhood we were in wasn't like ours. Dirt and trash were everywhere. Houses had rusted gates surrounding them like Lego pieces snapped tight and painted white. We weren't scared, though. Our neighborhood isn't so great either. And when you spend all your time in church, you feel safe even when you have to walk past crack houses to get where you're going.

Satina saw the boys first. Tall sweaty boys with muscles and big mouths, who pushed each other on the court, or yelled at one another from skinny wooden benches. Satina is prettier than the rest of us. She's five-foot one, with black hair and giant black eyes that make her look like a baby doll. So naturally the boys yelled for her first.

"Hey! You! Come here."

Daylea started pulling at her shorts, like she could make them longer. Satina stuck out her chest and smiled. "Okay," she said, taking me by the arm and heading their way.

My feet didn't move. Neither did K'ya's, Karen's, or anyone else's.

"We should leave," K'ya said.

My heart beat so fast I couldn't think.

"Too late to back out now," Satina said, swinging her hips and glossing her lips.

Jamaica is a tall, dark-skinned girl with long dark wavy hair that makes her look Indian sometimes. The boys could tell, I guess, 'cause one of them yelled for her, too.

"Yo, big girl!" he said. "Yeah, you," he said when she looked his way. "Come here."

Jamaica backed up. "Pastor's gonna be mad."

Daylea grabbed her hand. "Well, Pastor ain't here. And Pastor ain't fourteen, neither." She dug in her purse and pulled out square silver earrings as big as Pop Tarts. "He's old, and he's had his fun.

Now he wants to stop us from having ours." She pushed the earrings through the holes in her ears.

Satina looked mad when she said that. But what could she say? Daylea pulled Jamaica into the street. We all followed, breathing hard but not saying a word. Our eyes went from the boys to all them girls sitting in the stands watching them play.

"It's gonna be easy," Anna Belle said. "They already like us."

I stuck my chest out. K'ya pulled the rubber band off her hair and shook. Her brown hair jumped. China waved her finger like Pastor does when Daylea, N'kia, and K'ya started opening the top buttons on their shirts.

"You do that," Jamaica said, stopping right in the middle of the street, "and I'm gonna call Pastor right now."

We all believed her, so the buttons closed again, and our feet keep moving across the hot black asphalt.

"Yo, girlie," one boy said. He didn't have a shirt on. You could see sweat and dirt on his chest, and a ring in his nipple. K'ya pulled her shirt from out her skirt and tied it so her flat yellow belly showed.

Jamaica looked disgusted and started singing under her breath.

> *The devil knows what you like to do.*
> *The devil knows the good and bad that's in you.*
> *But the devil can't make you do what you do.*
> *You better act like you know the right way.*

Satina can't sing as good as Jamaica, but she's louder. So when she started rapping, and Daylea, K'ya, and even Anna Belle started clapping, they drowned Jamaica out.

> *So you say life is fun?*
> *Well, well, well,*
> *You can't prove it to this one.*
> *Well, well, well,*
> *All I do is what they say,*
> *Kneel down and pray,*
> *Go to church every day.*
> *Well, well, well,*
> *Lord, I love you, I swear I do,*
> *But can't my life have some fun in it too?*

We laughed when Jamaica covered Satina's

mouth and the words pushed through her fingers anyhow. "*I wanna dance with boys . . . yeah, you made them too, Lord. . . .*"

"Ouch," Jamaica said, looking at the bite mark on her hand. But Satina didn't care about the song no more. She was looking at the boy with the Z tattooed on her arm. "I want him."

I looked at her with her tight shorts, gold earrings with her name spelled on them, and sandals that showed off toenail polish we aren't allowed to wear.

Satina's doing everything wrong, I thought, *and she's the one all the boys want.*

Z looked Puerto Rican or Cuban. He was as brown as the edges on Sister Berta's walnut sugar cookies. He was tall too, maybe sixteen years old, with light brown hair that hung in his eyes and stuck to his sweaty brown neck.

"You like this, don't you?" he said to Satina, smacking his chest, then jumping high in the air and sending the ball into the hoop. "Yeah, you like it," he said, wiggling his long tongue at her.

Satina stared at him.

Anna Belle told her that wasn't no compliment he just gave her. "That was just nasty."

She was right. Me and Satina knew that.

But we kept our eyes on him anyway. "Sit down before you get knocked down," a girl said.

Being a pastor's kid, Satina doesn't always think the rules apply to her, 'cause everybody from the Church Mother to the janitor lets her have her way when she wants. So she just ignored the girl telling us to move and hollered at the boy with the Z tattoo.

"Hey. You. Come here," she said, like she fit right in. A few minutes later, Z was twisting one of her curls, and eyeing her all over.

China, Daylea, and me just watched and wished for somebody cute to come talk to us, too. But before they could, another girl yelled at us. "If you don't move your big head . . ."

I knew she was talking to me because I have the kind of head that you have to special-order hats for. So I moved out of her way and stared at the boy in the red tank top. "God's got somebody for everybody, right?" I asked Jamaica.

She rolled her eyes, then pointed to the court. "We ain't like them," she said. Then she pointed to the girls behind us. "Or them."

We headed for the bleachers and sat down. I looked at all them half-dressed girls sitting around us. Jamaica was right, I thought, we are not like *those* girls.

"What you looking at?" a girl in a gold halter top and no bra said.

I fixed my eyes on the game. "Nothing."

She stood up then. "Oh, so I'm nothing, huh?"

I didn't know what to say, so I didn't say anything.

"Get out the way!" another girl shouted to Satina and them. She, Daylea, and N'kia were still by the fence watching the game.

"GET! OUT! THE! WAY!"

Daylea and N'kia tripped over each other trying to make that girl happy. They came and sat down with us.

The gold halter top looked at me. "Why y'all here?"

We all looked to Jamaica. But Jamaica kept her mouth shut. So we did the same.

"You . . . You down there," a blond-haired girl said to Satina. "Get out his face."

Z smiled. Then told the girl to mind her business, 'cause he was sure minding his.

Satina was standing real close to him. He was whispering in her ear. Every once in a while she would giggle, but when she cut her eyes over to us, she looked kind of scared.

Anna Belle stood up. "We need to leave," she said, looking Jamaica's way. "'Cause God's not gonna bless no mess." She was repeating one of Sister Berta's lines.

K'ya called for Satina. I thought maybe she was gonna tell her it was time to go home. But she wanted to know if Z had a friend. "'Cause I wanna meet somebody, too."

Jamaica said they had ten minutes to do what they were gonna do because after that she was leaving this place.

"Go then," K'ya said, "because we came here on a mission."

Satina called for China, N'kia, K'ya, and Daylea to come over to the fence. When four big boys walked over to be with them, the girls behind us started whispering. No, not whispering, loud talking. Saying there was gonna be a beat-down 'round here if somebody didn't get out somebody else's face.

That's when the girl in the halter top leaned over and asked where we were from. I said Hilton Heights. Jamaica said the Calvary Church of God's Blessed Example. The girl pointed to Satina. "Her too?" She covered her mouth and laughed.

Before we could say anything, a girl ran past us talking about Satina. "I'm gonna kick her butt now!" she called to her friend.

Jamaica yelled for Satina. But before she could get her attention, two other girls were up in her face. They were cussing. Asking all five of 'em who they thought they were, coming in their neighborhood like they owned it.

The game never stopped. But more girls went over to the fence. And they got louder and meaner, and pushed harder. "Let's go," Jamaica said.

Karen, Anna Belle, and Lisa said they weren't going down there to get beat up, too. Jamaica said they were right. Wasn't no reason for all of us to get in a fight. But when we got to the pavement, Jamaica headed one way, and we headed the other. There was, like, sixteen girls gathered 'round Satina and them. And the boys were just egging them on.

"Yeah. Yeah, get that hair, so we can see if it's real," one said.

"Tear her top off and let's see what's under that shirt," Z laughed.

I looked at Jamaica. "Don't go, or they'll beat you up, too."

Her right hand trembled. "I asked God to stop

the fight before I get over there. But I don't think
he's gonna."

"Me neither," I said.

Jamaica headed for the fence all by herself. She
was singing, so I started singing, too.

> Lord, I am scared.
> Please don't hold it against me.
> God, I am weak.
> Please don't hold it against me.
> Please don't hold it against me when I do what
>   shouldn't.
> When I act like you don't,
> When I do what you wouldn't.

When they hit Jamaica in the face with a shoe,
me, Anna Bell, Lisa, and Karen run away like she
was a stranger. We didn't even wait for each other
once we got outside the hoop court. So I was by
myself when I got to the candy store two blocks
away and called Pastor. He was at home and we
were in trouble. I knew that before he even said one
word to me.

Our parents put us on punishment for six weeks.
When you don't have a TV, radio, or computer, like

most of us, what can they take off you? Nothing. So they put us to work in the church. They had us scrubbing walls and floors, polishing pews that hadn't been waxed in years, scouring pots, papering cabinets, stripping wax off floors, and erasing marks from leftover Bibles and ragged hymnals.

While that was happening, Satina's father came up with rules on how girls at our church should act. It was Satina's idea to write them down and post them in the church where everyone could see them all the time. So on the last Saturday of our six-week punishment, we wrote them in blue metallic ink and mounted them high on the basement wall where we hang out most of the time.

The Girls of the Calvary Church of God's Blessed Example Do Not:

1. Date
2. Wear lipstick, short skirts, tube tops, jewelry, or makeup
3. Dance, or go to activities outside the church
4. Disobey their parents
5. Hurt themselves or their families with negative and destructive behavior

Jamaica thought it was silly. Me too, kind of. "Writing the rules down won't make you obey them," she said.

Satina disagreed. "I knew them before," she said, painting silver stars on the poster, "but I think I'll follow them now for sure."

We looked at her. I'd keep to them too, I thought to myself, if I'd gotten hunks of my hair pulled out and my front tooth cracked, like she did.

"All right," Satina said, closing the bottle of paint. "We have to plan for Teen Sunday and show the elders how responsible we are."

"Yeah," China said. "We'll usher and read the announcements on Sunday, and go door-to-door all week long, raising money for something worthy— like old people."

Satina looked at her when she said that.

"What?" China asked.

"Nothing," Satina said, rubbing paint off her finger. But while China was telling us how much money we should raise and what cause to donate it to, Satina wrote me a note in shiny silver letters. "You think we'll meet some boys while we're out there?"

I stared at her. "Maybe," I said, eyeing the rules, then looking at the cross over the door.

Wanted: A Thug

Dear Girl with All the Answers @ Teen Queen Magazine:

I like my boyfriend, but I like my best friend's boyfriend better. Help!

You can call me Cheryl. I ain't gonna tell you my real name, 'cause if I do, my girls are gonna find out what I'm up to and jack me up. 'Cause there's two rules you don't break 'round where I live—you don't squeal, and you don't go sniffing after nobody's man.

Anyhow, don't let me get sidetracked. I'm fifteen years old. Me and my man been going together for two years. He is fine. Better than fine, really. I ain't giving you his real name here 'cause he would be hurt if he heard what I'm about to tell you. So let's just call him J. Anyhow, me and J been going together since seventh grade. He the boy that all the other girls want for their boyfriend. He on the basketball team. He on the baseball team and he got a job, too. He got pretty, light brown eyes, good hair, and good manners, unlike most boys his age. J opens doors for you. Says "Yes, ma'am," and "No, sir" to grown-ups. He always remembers my birthday. He the kind of boy everybody say is sooo nice. Well, that's the problem really. He's too nice. Boring, really. Why can't he be different? Like my girlfriend's boyfriend. He a thug. And more and more I been thinking, I want one of them, too.

Now, 'fore you start going off on me, let me tell you this. All thugs ain't bad. I mean, they ain't all out there playing girls and hanging out and making trouble. Some of 'em is nice, like my girlfriend Katherine's (not her real name) boyfriend, Rowl-D. He makes a girl want to lose her mind. All he got to do is look at you, and you be wanting to rob banks and knock old ladies over the head for him. He got sneaky little brown eyes that look at every girl like maybe they got a chance with him if only they play they cards right. He ain't tall, like J. He average height. He wears braids with a bandanna wrapped 'round his head, diamond hoop earrings, and designer clothes. He smokes, too. (That's the only thing I don't like.)

Now, I know what you thinking. Why I want to trade J for a boy like Rowl-D? Especially when Rowl-D's failing ninth grade, been kicked out the house by his parents, and don't treat my girlfriend like she really his? Well, I know it sounds stupid, but I think he's gonna be different with me. See, me and him been talking. My friend don't know it, but him and me been on the phone late at night after my parents go to sleep. And Rowl-D been telling me stuff. You know that boy been taking care of hisself since he was seven? And his momma ain't never been married, but she done lived with four men in the last six years? You'd be a thug too, if you was him.

Rowl-D says he likes nice girls. Quiet ones, like me. My girlfriend ain't quiet at all. She so loud that you can hear her down the hall when she talks. I asked Rowl-D, "How you get hooked up with her?" "I don't know," he said. "Guess you drink Pepsi if ain't no Coke around. But when the real good stuff show up, like you, then the crap gotta go. Know what I'm saying?"

I like that. Him calling me the real good stuff. I am, too. J knows that. That's why he be treating me so good. Only he boring. Don't want to do nothing but watch TV and play basketball. Rowl-D says he be clubbing. That if I was his girl he would hook me up with a ring, or necklace, or something. Miss Answers, did I say he ain't got no job? He wears chains so big 'round his neck, I wonder how he can stand up straight. But he say he ain't never worked. He got connections. That's kind of scary, you know. Kind of exciting too. Is it wrong for me to like that about him? I hope not.

I told Rowl-D that I feel bad about him and me talking behind my friend's back. He told me not to worry. He gonna dump her soon. "Then it's you and me. All right?"

I don't know. Katherine is my friend. We been tight since elementary school. When she first met Rowl-D, I told her not to have nothing to do with him. "He trash," I said. Now here I am, dreaming 'bout that boy. Sneaking 'round after school just so I can be with him. The other day I came in so late my father took the belt to me. Rowl-D and me wasn't doing nothing. Just talking. For real. Thugs know how to hold a conversation too, you know.

Anyhow, I'm writing you for a lot of reasons. Do you think I should tell my friend Katherine what's going on? And what about J—would you dump him if you was me? Most important of all, do you think a girl like me stands a chance with a thug? I mean, some of the people Rowl-D run with is in gangs and stuff. Most of 'em been kicked out of school, or just stopped going. But not Rowl-D. He a thug, but he got potential. He say that somebody like me make him want to do right. I think he's right about that. What you think?

Can't wait for you to answer me,

Melody

Dear Melody:

Sorry, but your letter won't ever appear in Teen Queen magazine.

I pulled it as soon as I read it. I stashed it in

my purse and took it home with me. That's
against the rules, you know. But I don't care.
'Cause if I had published your letter, your girls
woulda beat the crap outta you, and everybody
at school would know what kind of girl you
really are.

You see, I know you. (You signed your real
name at the end of your letter.) I'm in two of your
classes. I'm not telling you my name. That's a
secret I can't reveal. But I am in eleventh grade at
John Marshall High. I lucked out six months ago
and got picked to write for Teen Queen magazine.
This is the first time I broke the magazine's
rules, though. But to me, it's worth getting caught,
and maybe fired, to let you know where I'm
coming from.

You probably think you're the only girl with
this problem. You're not. Recently we got a letter
just like yours. But the editors didn't include
this girl's letter in the magazine. They say girls
take other girls' boyfriends all the time. But I
figure you can learn a thing or two from her. So
here goes.

I can't give you her real name so I'll call her

Shavon. Anyhow, Shavon attended five different high schools before coming to ours. You'd think somebody was chasing her, huh? Well, they were. A whole gang of girls—who were better than dope-sniffing dogs when it came to tracking people down—showed up every place she went.

Things for her started out the same way they did with you. She liked her best friend's boyfriend. He was so cute, the girls nicknamed him Pretty. She wasn't looking to take him from her girlfriend, either. It's just that one day Pretty came up to her when her friend Cassandra was home sick with the cramps. It was after school and nobody else was around. You know boys. He got closer to Shavon than he should. Said all the right things. Then he kissed her. Naturally, she kissed him back. Wouldn't you?

You know, Melody, girls like you and Shavon always end up the same—chasing some boy who already got some other girl chasing behind him too. Anyhow, Shavon decided she wanted Pretty all to herself. So she started writing anonymous letters to Cassandra, telling her she'd better watch her man because he was stepping out on her.

Shavon figured Cassandra would dump Pretty.
But Cassandra wasn't letting go of her man that
easily. So she got her friends together and asked
them what was up. She followed Pretty everywhere he went. That's when Pretty told Shavon
him and her had to chill. And that's when Shavon
really screwed things up. Putting notes every place
Cassandra went—in her locker, under her desk,
and stuffed in her sneakers just before she put 'em
on for gym. Making it so Cassandra wouldn't let
Pretty out of her sight.

Shavon and Pretty didn't hang together after
that. They started arguing and fighting. That's
when she let it slip that she was the one who wrote
the notes. You'd think a boy like Pretty woulda
slapped her silly. He didn't. But he got even with
her anyhow. He told Cassandra what she did, and
Cassandra came after Shavon. She hit her in the
head with a geometry book. But that was just the
beginning. For the rest of the year, she kept it
coming. Her friends called Shavon's house almost
every hour on the hour for six months. Even after
her parents changed phone numbers for the fourth
time. They drove by her house and hit it with raw

eggs, rotten chicken, bags of garbage. They
scratched up her dad's ride. They stole her little
sister's bike. They chased her home from the park,
from the pool, from the bus stop, the mall, the
movie theater—everywhere and everyplace
she went.

Sometimes when Cassandra or her girls came
after Shavon, she'd see Pretty's ride waiting. For a
long, long time she said she was madder at him
than at Cassandra. But then she said she finally
figured it out. She didn't have a right to be mad
at him or her. "I invited all that drama in my life
by digging in somebody else's trash. So why should
I be pissed off 'cause maggots got all over me?"

Melody, I'm telling you this so you don't end
up like Shavon—dogging your girl and chasing a
boy that ain't gonna respect you one bit when it's
all said and done. But that ain't the only reason
I'm spilling my guts. There's another reason too.
See, I know the girl whose man you're trying to
take. He ain't worth two cents. But she likes
him—loves him even. And since she's my sister,
the baby of our family, I gotta look out for her.
Right? And well, I ain't gonna let nobody do

her wrong. So consider yourself warned. Get out from under Rowl-D, 'fore things start happening to you. Bad things. The kind of things that happened to me. And you already know from this here letter that I ain't forgot one thing that was done to me by them girls. And you know what? You won't never forget what I do to you, neither. Yours truly,

The Girl with All the Answers

Not a Boy

"**H**OW I LOOK, MAN?" I say, checking myself out in the mirror.

My friend Richard throws a comb at me. "Why you doing all this, man? She ain't even cute."

I wanna clock him. He been busting on my girl, Yesterday, for two hours now. Just jealous, I say to myself.

Richard finishes off the pickle-and-tuna sandwich that's been sitting on my dresser for the last hour. "Simone and Jasmine look better than Yesterday. You shoulda asked one of them out."

It took me half the year to get Yesterday to go out with me. She's a quiet girl. You say hi to her and she stares at the floor and says hi so low you can't hardly hear her. But she's pretty. And for four months now, we been lab partners in chemistry class. You gotta talk in that class.

"Cecil," my mother yells up the steps. "Don't you be late picking that girl up."

I swallow, unbutton my shirt, and dump powder on my chest.

Richard says I smell like his sister. I pop him upside the head.

"Cecil!" my dad shouts. "If you don't . . ."

I take one last look at myself in the mirror. Nice, I think.

Richard shakes his head. "You pathetic, man. Never been on a date. Got your dad driving you to some girl's house."

Richard thinks he knows everything. But he's wrong this time. I mean, I been on group dates. Library dates. Supposed-to-be-at-choir-rehearsal-but-sneaking-off-with-a-cutie-all-by-myself dates. But when I turned fifteen two months ago, my dad said I could go on a real date. I been asking Yesterday out all this time. She been telling me no. Then I just came out and told her: "I like you, a lot; better than any girl ever." I sounded so corny. But I got to her, I guess. 'Cause three days later she said, "Okay. We can go to the movies."

By the time I get downstairs, my father is asking me a million goofy questions. Did I brush my teeth? Do I have mints in case the popcorn stinks up my breath? Do I have enough money? I ain't even listening to him. I'm thinking 'bout the flowers my mother bought for me to give to Yesterday. I hid 'em this morning.

"Fellas don't do that no more," I tell her when she asks about them.

"My boy does," she says, shoving six red roses she takes out of a vase in the middle of the dining-room table at me.

Richard shakes his head. "Don't do it, man," he says, walking out the front door.

My father pats his pockets for car keys. "You a man now, not a boy. Gotta act like one," he says, taking the flowers off my mom and handing them to me. I throw 'em on the couch on my way out the door.

"My boy . . . a man," he says, when we get in the car. Then he leans over and stares at my mouth. "Sure you brushed? Teeth look kinda yella."

I turn the rearview mirror my way. Scratch some white, cheeselike stuff off my teeth. Throw open the car door and tell my dad that I'll be right back. I brush my teeth twice. I gargle. I think about

Yesterday. How I like her hair—light brown and straight down to her shoulders. How I like her eyes, even though you can't hardly see them behind her glasses.

"Boy? You coming or what?" my mother shouts.

I run down the steps, out the door, and into the car. The roses are sitting on the dashboard tied together with a ribbon. For a minute, I think about tossing 'em out the window.

My dad starts the engine. "Who would name a child Yesterday?"

I don't answer. Kids tease her all the time about her name.

"I mean, who would do that to a child?" he says, backing out the driveway. "Shoulda just named her Tomorrow, or Next Tuesday, for goodness' sake."

I stare out the window. I don't care what her name is. She's fine. I like her.

I point out the window and tell my father to turn left. He stops at the light. "I'm gonna go to the door with you," he says. "Meet her folks. Let 'em know you come from quality, too."

"No!"

He lets me know this wasn't his idea. It was my mother's.

I take off my seat belt and look him right in the eye when I turn his way. "She ain't here. Anyhow, you ain't always gotta do what she says."

My father used to be a boxer. He still pumps iron every day and does 250 push-ups before work. But when it comes to my mother, he's a wuss. He does whatever she says. "Give the girl the flowers. It will make your mother happy."

I pick up the flowers. Pluck petals off one by one and throw 'em out the window. "I *said* I'm not taking her *no* flowers."

My father doesn't understand. My boys are already on me for not making her pay her own way. For going by her house to meet her folks instead of making her meet me at the movies, like they all do. They teasing me in school for walking her to class and sitting with her at lunch. I can't have her saying I gave her flowers. No.

My dad laughs. "Well, if she wants flowers, guess her daddy's gonna have to buy her some."

I'm glad he sees things my way. He steps on the gas. The car is doing 50 in a 25-mile zone. I put my seat belt back on. "Her parents are strict."

He looks at me. "You sure they don't wanna meet me?"

I don't answer. I sit back in my seat and shut my mouth for the rest of the ride.

Twenty minutes later we pull onto her block. "Thirty-seven eighteen, that's the address," I say, pointing to the house.

The front door opens wide. A woman with her hands on her hips stares at me. A man—a really tall, dark-skinned man—looks at me like he don't like me already.

My father makes his shoulder muscles jump, like her dad can see them from his front door. "I better go with ya."

I swallow. "I'm . . . I'm all right." I open the door, but I stay in my seat. I look over at the roses. My father pulls out the stem with no petals left and drops it on the floor. He tightens the orange ribbon holding the flowers together and hands them to me. "Sometimes," he says, "it's best not to be empty-handed."

I take the flowers, 'cause if I don't, my father will keep after me about them. Just like he won't quit talking about wanting to meet her folks. He's like that—once something gets in his head, he won't turn it loose until you give in and do things his way.

I look at Yesterday's dad, and I don't move.

My father turns the radio on low. The music is for elevators, not for a car with a man who bench-presses 450 and eats six eggs a day. "Yesterday. That's an interesting name."

I tell him that Yesterday got her name from her great, great, great-grandmother, who was a slave. Yesterday don't like it, though.

"But you like her, huh?" he asks.

I keep a lot of stuff to myself. Like how Yesterday stays in my head even when I'm asleep. Like how I wanna knock Jason Crews's teeth out for looking at her like he do sometimes. "She aiight," I tell my father. Then I see her peeking out the window, and my heart speeds up, and my throat gets tight, and I'm hot all over.

My father leans on the steering wheel. "All right, boy. Now, remember what I said."

I remember. Pay for everything—even the bus ride to and from the movies. Let her pick the seats. "If they're too close to the screen or too far away, keep quiet," my father said. "A girl likes to think a boy is considerate that way." Keep my hands to myself—maybe. And thank her for a nice evening. "If she's like your momma," he said, "she's got a diary.

And twenty years from now—whether you're with her or not—she's gonna read about what you did, and think you were the best thing that ever happened to her."

My father clears his throat. "You sure you don't want me to go in with you?"

"No!" I lower my voice. "You always telling me what to do . . . how to act. A *man* don't need his father holding his hand and telling him stuff all the time, now do he?"

I don't know where that came from. But I'm glad I said it. 'Cause my father is like my mother— always up in my business.

"Boy . . ."

I slap my chest hard. "I'm not a boy," I shout. "I'm a man." Right then, Yesterday's front door slams shut.

"Aaah, man," I say, throwing the flowers down. "Now see what you did?" I slam my door closed. "Ruined everything."

Me and my father both stare at the front door of the house, like we can open it with our eyes. He apologizes. I don't want to hear it. I shoulda took a bus. Only, buses don't run around here, so my father brought me . . . like I'm a little boy.

My father picks the roses off the floor and puts them in between us. I can tell he don't know what to do right now. Then he tells me again about the first time he took my mother out. "Her father met me at the front door with a two-page letter."

I say what comes next, 'cause I figure that way I can shorten the story. "It had the same two sentences written over and over again."

Me and my father say the words together. "'This is my daughter: if you do anything to make her cry, anything to disrespect her, anything to make people gossip about her or treat her differently, *you will live to regret it.* This is *my* daughter, *my* love, *my* heart—if you do anything to break *my* heart, I will make you pay over and over again.'"

I always laugh at that story, only now that I'm sitting outside Yesterday's door with her dad inside, maybe hating me, the words don't seem so funny no more. "Were you . . . were you scared when you met him?"

My father smiles. "Sure! You gotta be scared when you get something like that from a man who ain't smiling at you, and didn't shake your hand when you extended it."

I look at Yesterday's front door. "People don't do stuff like that no more."

He squeezes my shoulder. "That's his daughter. A man will hurt somebody over his baby girl."

I open the car door and put one foot on the pave-ment. "What if he don't open the door again?" I reach for the roses. Step out the car. Lean down and tell my father I'll see him later. I don't move, though. I keep thinking that maybe her father won't let me in the house. Or he'll open the door and curse me out or something. "Go," I tell myself, shutting the car door and walking up the steps. I'm thinking about my grandfather's letter. About Yesterday's dad. He wasn't big like my dad, but he looked mean—ugly too.

The roses in my hand are shaking like the wind's blowing out here. But it's just me, nervous enough to pee.

I shoulda done like Richard said, I think, and asked Jasmine or Simone out. They meet you any-where you want, so you ain't got to worry 'bout their father's going off on you.

When I knock on the door, nobody answers. I knock again. Nobody answers. I'm staring at my feet. Holding tight to the flowers. Not wanting to look back at my father . . . not wanting no more help from him. My fist is balled when I knock the next time, and I pound on the door harder than I want. I look at my watch. I been here, like, ten minutes. You blew it, man, I think. She ain't never going out with you now.

I'm thinking 'bout my boys. What they would say. *Forget her, man. There're more legs where hers come from.*

"Yeah, forget her," I say out loud. But then, I don't know, I knock on the door again.

The door flies open. "What?" It's her dad. "*What* do you want?"

I swallow. Clear my throat and try to remember my name.

"*Can I help you with something?*" he says, loud-talking me. "You sat in the car so long, I figured you'd changed your mind."

I don't have no words; no spit left neither, so my throat hurts like fingernails been scratching inside it.

"Do you want something here, boy?" her dad says. "If you do, speak up!"

Yesterday's dad and me stare at each other like men do sometimes when they ain't sure what the other's gonna do next. His hands start to push the door closed again. Then, finally, the words do come.

"Mr. Johnson, my name is Cecil. Cecil Carson. And this is my son," my dad says, walking up the steps and standing next to me.

Like that, I can breathe again. I reach out and shake Mr. Johnson's hand. I almost scream the words at first. "I'm Cecil Carson the Second, and I'm here for your daughter," I say, looking him *right* in the eyes.

A Letter to My Daughter

Dear Alicia,

I ain't the type to write letters. You know that. But, well, sometimes a man's gotta do what he don't like. So, I'm taking pen to paper, hoping you and your mother don't catch no spelling errors or find nothing wrong in here.

You're almost fifteen. Man. That's a lot of birthdays I done missed. But, well, the other day I seen you walking into the house. You looked so sweet. And the boys, I seen 'em looking. High-fiving each other when you walked by—saying what they would like to do to you.

I know I been gone too long to start playing daddy, but, girl, I had to get myself from around there quick, because I was ready to hurt somebody.

What you doing following me? That's what you asking yourself, huh? What you doing trying to get up in my life now, when you been gone for always? Good questions. Wish I had good answers. But it's just that I woke up this morning and, well, you was on my mind like an overdue bill. I wondered if you thought I done you wrong by never being around. Then I got to thinking about your momma, and what she tells you about me. Did she tell you I lived in a house not far from yours? That I finally got a steady job and a little change in my pocket? I'll admit it. I always liked life free and easy. Living in a different city every six months, that was me. Working long enough to earn a few dollars, buy some nice clothes, take some pretty woman to dinner and a movie, and hop another Greyhound outta town.

It's been almost a year now, and I'm still on the same job. Girl, it's killing me to stay put like regular folks. But it's time I planted some kinda roots, I guess. Anyhow, I got me a room in some old woman's house, who cooks just as good as your grandma. But me ain't why I'm writing to you.

So I'll stop here telling you how I'm doing.

Anyhow, I seen a man on television last week.
He said he was gonna leave his daughter the house,
the car, and $10,000 in his will when he died.
What I'm gonna leave my child? I thought. "Hard
times and heartbreak," I said to myself.

I couldn't stop thinking 'bout you, though. So I
came down last week and just watched you walk
with your head high and your mind on something
bigger than the mess all around you. You like your
momma, I swear you is. She was gonna be somebody.
Everybody said that. Then she met me. And I
talked her outta all her dreams, all her money, and
all her good sense too.

But what's in us don't just evaporate like steam
from hot pipes. That's what my mother used to say
anyhow. It lingers, like sediment (your momma
taught me them words), and every now and then it
turns into what it was meant to be in the first
place. So when I seen you, I saw your momma—
a tall, smart, big-boned beauty queen—living in
the jungle, fighting off tigers.

After I seen you, I went home and cried. Then I
wondered, do your momma cry, too? Do she know

you gonna turn out just like her—holding on too
long to a man who's gonna rip off her future and
make her regret the past?

You know, last night I dreamed about you.
You was living with your momma. You had two or
three babies, wasn't married, and didn't have no
idea where the daddies were. You watched
Jeopardy!, just like she used to. You played chess
and knew all the answers to The Price is Right.
But you was trapped, like her. "It's my fault!" I
yelled the words so loud in my sleep that night,
Mrs. Carson came into my room and woke
me up.

"If it's your fault, make it right," she said, not
even asking me what I was taking the blame for.

So today I came back again. Trying to figure
out how I could make things better for you. I ain't
got no money—just a hundred bucks saved. I got
no home to leave you when I die, neither. But
when I saw them wolves at the door, sniffing and
licking their lips, I figured I could leave you with
a little something. Knowledge. Not the stuff you
get from schoolbooks or National Geographic on
TV. Street stuff. Boy stuff. Knowledge that your

momma coulda used to take a different route through life.

So here goes. These's things I figure you need to know when it comes to boys. But don't go thinking I'm just gonna tell you how no good and miserable they is. Or how to avoid them. You already know some of that. I'm gonna tell you about how to separate the plums from the prunes. 'Cause it ain't just that girls don't pick the right guy. Shoot. They can't even recognize the wrong ones when they come along.

Anyhow, enough preaching. Time for some teaching, as my daddy used to say.

First off, remember this: Boys ain't girls. Most don't wanna know 'bout how you feel and what you think. They wanna get what they can from you and then move on. Then they wanna talk to their friends 'bout how things went for 'em. It's like hunting—once you shoot a deer, how you gonna keep that to yourself? The best part of the hunt, besides shooting the thing, is telling how you tricked it into doing what you wanted. How easy the whole thing was.

Second: Don't get all excited if some boy is

nice to you. Ain't the mailman nice to you? And what about your teachers, the drunk on the corner, or the little boy up the street? Nice ain't nothing much. Shoot, I'm nice to the snaggletoothed woman who scrubs the floors where I work. You think I wanna date her?

Let me get back to the point. Alicia, you deserve a boy who is more than nice to you. Women be thinking nice is enough. It ain't. It's a low bar to set for yourself. You deserve a boy who's gonna respect you. To get somebody like that though, you gotta know what you want. You smart. Write something down. Come up with a map that's gonna help lead you to the kind of fellow you want. They made us do that kind of stuff in school. Said, to get a job, we needed to be specific. To say—I want a job with benefits, that pays $150 a week, where I can get a fifteen-minute break twice a day.

Girls like you better do the same. How 'bout this: I want a boy who don't curse around me, goes to church, do what his momma says, goes to class all the time, and don't steal, or sell drugs. Okay, so maybe that's the kind of boy I want for you, but you see what I'm saying. Know what you want just as well as you know what you don't want. And don't settle for less, or one day you gonna regret it. Just ask your momma.

Third: If boys didn't have eyes, they'd make some for themselves. You see, boys/men like to look. And they like looking at women more than anything. So when you wear your short skirts and your low-cut tops, don't forget that what's hanging out is there for everybody to see. That means good and bad alike is gonna be taking inventory of what's yours. And just like in the stockroom where I work, some folk take better inventory than others. Some look from afar to see what's what. Others come in close, touch and feel and sniff and leave the shelf all discombobulated once they gone. You getting me? Maybe not. So I'll make it plain. A short skirt and a low-cut top is a man's best friend. So when you're wearing them (and you got a right to), don't think he's asking for your phone number just 'cause he thinks you're nice or smart or gonna make a good wife. He got other ideas. That's just how we is.

Fourth: There's some strong, good boys out

there. I see them. I knew them. I was one once.
But a girl's gotta make up her mind early that's
what she wants. And when the good ones come,
like spring water to a dry creek, don't be sticking
up your nose and saying how you know he ain't the
one 'cause he act silly, can't dance, or don't hang
with the cool kids at school. Baby girl, when you
measuring a boy, a man, you better use a different
kind of stick—not just one that tells you how
popular he is. But one that can poke around his
insides and see what's in his heart, his head, and
his habits.

Fifth: A good man will do just about anything for a good woman. Y'all gals got more power
over us than you think. But you so scared that you
gonna lose us if you don't do like we say, you forget
how strong you are. So you give us what we
want—your body, your cash, the time you should
be spending on the books or with your girlfriends,
even your mind. When I seen you, you was walking tall, like your back was made out of 100-
year-old pine. Stay that way. Men like to know
that a tree don't bend easy as a piece of paper.

Six: A boy's father shows him how to be a

man, so watch out for boys whose fathers are missing in action. It don't mean them boys don't know how to be men. Shoot, some know how better than others. But it mean you need to do some extra checking, deeper thinking. Do the boy know how to work hard for what he wants in life? Do he beep the horn for you or walk up to the front door and knock like he got a queen waiting for him? Do he know how to hold back his nature? I'm being real now. 'Cause a man will teach a boy (if he half a man) to be selective. Do he know that real men don't hit women? Do he know that what's between him and you is between him and you—not him, you, and all his friends? Look, girl! Ask questions! Don't be afraid he gonna leave you, 'cause, more likely than not, y'all gonna break up in a few months anyhow. Shoot! This ain't no Disney film. It's real life. And there's plenty of hurt out there for you if you don't think smart and toughen up a little.

Seven: Boys need girls to help them feel like men. Oh, they be acting like they don't need y'all. Acting like all they want is what they can get. But girls make boys feel like manhood is worth

the trip. It's not just 'cause y'all pretty and sweet
and soft as roses. Y'all complete 'em, honey. Make
us feel like we can do anything. So when you do
date, remember that. Don't go screaming at them
in front of folks. Don't go putting their business
in the street. Help him to be better than he ever
thought he could be—but don't go losing pieces of
yourself doing it. Stay whole, and let him stay
whole too. And then, if you do break up, there's
gonna be another boy/man out there looking out
for you, believing in you too.

Eight: Every girl needs a warrior—a boy, or
man, who's got her back. No, not some thug who
spends all his time looking for or causing trouble.
But a strong man—inside and out. I ain't always
been that for you, but I want it for you anyhow. In
the movies, warriors carry big shields, so when
rocks and arrows come, they protected, and so is the
people they love. That's what you want in a
boy/man—somebody who will stop the rocks.
Somebody who won't sit still while you get called
a ho or a B, or something else you know you ain't.
Somebody who knows right, wants to do right, and
will fight for right when it comes your way.

Alicia, a warrior ain't just strong arms and fists, though. He's a thinker. A hard worker. Somebody who's willing to do without, to make sure his own is taken care of. I used to be a warrior when I was young like you. But somewhere, I forgot that was one of my jobs too.

Nine: Boys is nice, so is men, but sometimes it's just you and you. So if you ain't got a boyfriend, remember you still got you. You still got your dreams, your talent, and your smarts. Your momma used to dance ballet in school. And she always was in some kind of play, or running for office. She ever tell you she was school president? All that stuff's in you too. So let it out and don't bury it for nobody. 'Cause you is so much more than a pretty face and a tight pair of jeans, some boy's girlfriend or some man's wife.

Ten: No matter what kind of advice a man gives a girl, she gonna choose the wrong road, for a little while anyhow. So if you forget who you is, and end up with a knuckleheaded boy, don't think you obligated to stay put. You got feet, don't you? And a mind, right? So correct the situation. Be gone. Remember, a strong girl knows when she gone up the wrong street, and she ain't ashamed to back out, make a U-turn, and start again. Your momma taught me that. It took her way too long, but she saved herself and you in the end. You gotta do that sometimes.

Well, I can't think of nothing more to say. Anyhow, it's late and my fingers is tired. I swear they is. But I'm hoping you gonna see some good in what's wrote here. It ain't $10,000 or a house you can lay your head in. But it's a future for you nonetheless. A way out, if you take it. A map that might just lead you to a pretty good place.

Alicia, this is all I got to offer. I'm hoping you'll take it and do right by what's here. 'Cause Daddy loves you, girl. And he wanna make sure he don't ruin no more futures, especially yours.

—Daddy

(the first man who ever loved you)